THE USBORNE
INTERNET-LINKED
INTRODUCTION TO
ASIA

Elizabeth Dalby

Designed by Joanne Kirkby, Karen Tomlins,
Candice Whatmore and Kate Rimmer

Digital imagery by Keith Furnival and Joanne Kirkby

Edited by Kirsteen Rogers

Consultants: Professor Michael Hitchcock, London Metropolitan University
and Professor Ulrich Kratz, School of Oriental and African Studies

Cartography: European Map Graphics Ltd

Consultant cartographic editor: Craig Asquith

Internet links

Throughout this book, we have suggested interesting websites where you can find out more about Asia. To visit the sites, go to the Usborne Quicklinks Website at www.usborne-quicklinks.com and type the keyword "asia". There you will find links to click on to take you to all the sites. Here are some of the things you can do on the websites:

- Take a snapshot tour of India's incredible landscapes and wildlife.

- Follow the tea trail to find out how tea is produced, and then try a tea-related crossword, quiz and wordsearch.

- Explore the Kamchatka Peninsula and meet some of the creatures that live there.

INTERNET LINK

For a link to a website with an introduction to Japanese calligraphy, and a chance to try virtual calligraphy, go to **www.usborne-quicklinks.com**

Look for descriptions of recommended websites on the pages of this book, then go to the Usborne Quicklinks Website for links to all the sites.

Internet safety

When using the Internet, please follow these guidelines:

- Ask your parent's or guardian's permission before you connect to the Internet.

- If you write a message in a website guest book or on a website message board, do not include any personal information such as your full name, address or telephone number, and ask an adult before you give your email address.

- If a website asks you to log in or register by typing your name or email address, ask permission of an adult first.

- If you do receive an email from someone you don't know, tell an adult and do not reply to the email.

- Never arrange to meet anyone you have talked to on the Internet.

Note for parents and guardians

The websites described in this book are regularly reviewed and the links in Usborne Quicklinks are updated. However, the content of a website may change at any time and Usborne Publishing is not responsible for the content on any website other than its own.

We recommend that children are supervised while on the Internet, that they do not use Internet chat rooms, and that you use Internet filtering software to block unsuitable material. Please ensure that your children read and follow the safety guidelines printed on the left. For more information, see the "Net Help" area on the Usborne Quicklinks Website.

Site availability

The links in Usborne Quicklinks are regularly reviewed and updated, but occasionally you may get a message that a site is unavailable. This might be temporary, so try again later, or even the next day. If any of the sites close down, we will, if possible, replace them with suitable alternatives, so you will always find an up-to-date list of sites in Usborne Quicklinks.

Computer not essential

If you don't have access to the Internet, don't worry. This book is a complete, self-contained reference book on its own.

Contents

Lanterns for the Chinese New Year festival hang outside a shop in Vietnam. They symbolize long life and good luck.

Two Indian women lay newly dyed cotton fabric out to dry in the hot sun, in the desert region of Rajasthan.

Introduction to Asia

Asia is by far the biggest continent in the world. It contains every kind of landscape, from ice and snow to scorched, arid deserts, and from windswept grasslands to lush, tropical rainforests, as well as many of the Earth's highest mountain ranges. Asia is made up of around 50 countries, including some of the world's largest and most densely populated. Over half of all the people on Earth live in Asia, and their religions, cultures, languages and traditions have a huge influence across the world.

In this book, the continent of Asia has been divided into regions, shown on the map over the page. Each section begins with an introduction to the region and a map of the countries in it. Read on to find out about the area's landscapes, climate, crops and wildlife, as well as its natural resources and environmental issues. You can also take a look at the people who live there – their towns and cities, their religions, art, culture, entertainment and everyday life.

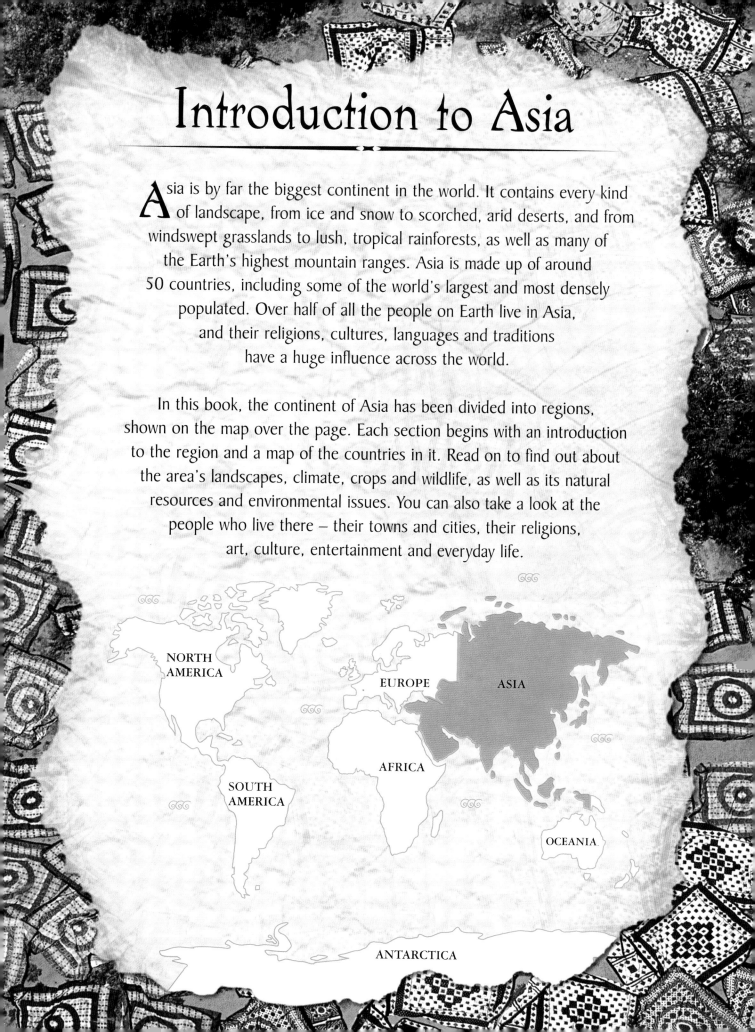

NORTH AMERICA

EUROPE

ASIA

SOUTH AMERICA

AFRICA

OCEANIA

ANTARCTICA

Map of Asia

All the countries that make up Asia are shown on this map, as well as capital cities and the names of seas and oceans. The map has been shaded to show the different regions that are featured in this book.

Key to map of Asia

- ■   Capital city
- ----   Boundary between Asia and Europe
- ▬▬   Borders between countries
- ──   Coastlines
- ▨   Lakes and inland seas
- ໑໑໑   Seas
- ∿   Rivers

0km   1,000km
0 miles   640 miles

Central Asia

Central Asia includes Kazakhstan, Turkmenistan, Uzbekistan, Kyrgyzstan, Tajikistan, Afghanistan and Mongolia. Mongolia is a little way to the east of the other countries in the region, but the people living there share a similar way of life with the people in the other Central Asian countries.

The Indian Subcontinent

The Indian Subcontinent includes India, Pakistan, Nepal, Bhutan, Bangladesh, Sri Lanka and the Maldives. These countries are separated from the rest of Asia to the north by enormous mountain ranges.

There are more detailed, regional maps of Asia on pages 74–85, showing many more towns and cities as well as mountains, rivers and other types of landscapes.

Russia

Russia is the largest country in Asia and although a small part of it is actually in Europe, the whole country is included in this book. Moscow, Russia's capital, is in the European part, and things that happen there often affect the country as a whole. As it is part of both continents, Russia considers itself both Asian and European.

Eastern Asia

Eastern Asia includes China, Japan, North Korea, South Korea and Taiwan. Japan, Taiwan and North and South Korea have all been influenced by China's culture and way of life.

Mainland Southeast Asia

Mainland Southeast Asia includes Laos, Burma (Myanmar), Vietnam, Thailand and Cambodia. These countries share similar cultures and languages, and the Buddhist faith is an important part of everyday life.

Maritime Southeast Asia

Maritime Southeast Asia includes Malaysia, Indonesia, the Philippines, Singapore, East Timor and Brunei. These countries form a vast group of islands that spread across the South China Sea, to the south and east of mainland Asia.

The Middle East

The countries shown in white make up the region known as the Middle East and are not covered in this book.

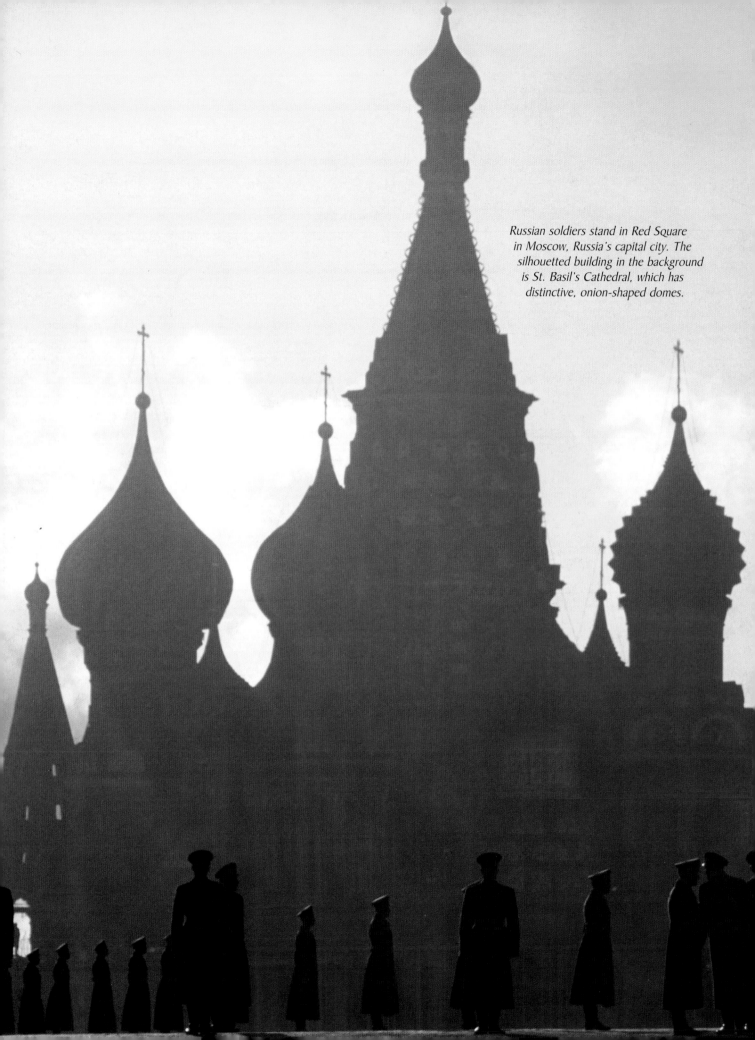

Russian soldiers stand in Red Square in Moscow, Russia's capital city. The silhouetted building in the background is St. Basil's Cathedral, which has distinctive, onion-shaped domes.

Russia

Russia is by far the biggest country in the world and it takes seven days to cross it by train. The smaller part of Russia to the west of the Ural Mountains is in Europe, but the much larger, eastern part stretches across all of northern Asia. Eastern Russia is often called Siberia.

Siberia is notoriously cold. Almost all of Russia's northern coast is inside the Arctic Circle, and most of the land farther south is covered in freezing forest. Where southern Russia meets the countries of Central Asia, the forest gives way to rolling, windswept grasslands and fields of wheat and cotton.

Siberian snowscapes

Freezing forests

Much of northern Russia is covered in *taiga* forest. The word *taiga* comes from Russian and is used to describe cold, evergreen forests. Russia's *taiga* is the largest forested area in the world – twice as big as the Amazon rainforest in South America. Despite the freezing climate, many animals live in the *taiga*, including brown bears, snow leopards and Siberian tigers. But the *taiga* is shrinking, as trees are cut down for timber. Even if trees are replanted, the climate is so cold that the new trees take many years to grow.

This snowy pine forest is in Yakutia, in the far northeastern corner of Russia, near the Verkhoyansk mountains. Very few people live in this isolated area.

A group of Russian boys has cleared a patch of snow away from the frozen surface of Lake Baikal, for a game of ice hockey.

Lake Baikal

The deepest lake on Earth is Lake Baikal, in southern Siberia. If the lake were emptied, it would take 400 years for the rivers that flow into it to fill it again. The huge amount of water in Lake Baikal affects the climate near its shores, because water heats up and cools down much more slowly than land does. Near the lake, the summers are cooler and the winters are milder than they are in the rest of Siberia. Even so, in winter, the lake freezes over with a layer of ice thick enough to skate on or even drive across.

INTERNET LINK

For a link to a website where you can find out about the volcanic wilderness of the Kamchatka Peninsula in eastern Russia, go to **www.usborne-quicklinks.com**

The Arctic north

The extreme northern fringe of Russia's land, deep inside the Arctic Circle, is tundra – a flat, marshy, treeless plain, lashed by biting winds. The ground there contains a thick layer called permafrost that stays frozen solid all year round. This prevents large plants and trees from taking root.

Creatures that live on the tundra include many species of tiny flies and mosquitoes. There are also small mammals, such as ground squirrels and lemmings, and much larger mammals like caribou and musk oxen. These large tundra animals are always on the move, trying to find new pastures that they can raid for food.

Arctic ground squirrels live on the Siberian tundra, where they search for grasses, mushrooms and berries to eat.

Kamchatka Peninsula

The Kamchatka Peninsula sticks out from Russia like a tongue, into the Pacific Ocean. It's an area of stunning natural wilderness with many active, rumbling volcanoes, bubbling hot springs and erupting jets of hot water called geysers. The mountains are carved into jagged shapes by slowly flowing rivers of ice called glaciers. This region is one of the most active parts of a huge, arc-shaped zone of volcanoes that surrounds the Pacific Ocean.

This rocky crater, on one of the volcanoes on the Kamchatka Peninsula, is partly filled by a brilliant blue-green lake, which is heated by volcanic activity from below.

Beliefs and lifestyles

Orthodox Christianity

Many Russians are Orthodox Christians. Orthodox churches are adorned with gold decorations and icons – painted pictures of saints. Peals of bells call people to lavish church ceremonies which include rituals such as burning candles, and are accompanied by passionate singing. During the 20th century, Russia's Communist leaders discouraged all religions, but Orthodox Christianity survived, and today it is becoming more popular once again.

Onion-shaped domes are typical of Russian Orthodox churches like this, the Church of the Transfiguration on Kizhi Island, near Moscow. The domes were originally designed to allow snow to fall off easily in Russia's cold climate.

Links with Mongolia

A part of Siberia, south of Lake Baikal, is home to many Buryat people. It was once part of the vast Mongolian empire, which stretched from central Asia to China. Many people there share beliefs with people living in present-day Mongolia, such as Buddhism and shamanism (spirit worship), and they also wear similar traditional costumes.

These Siberian girls are wearing traditional summer costumes, similar to those worn by people living in Mongolia and parts of China.

This man belongs to a group of people called the Nenets, who live in Siberia. He is leading a caravan of reindeer, and is warmly dressed in a coat made of reindeer fur.

Reindeer herders

In Russia's far north live the Nenets people. They are reindeer herders who travel across the tundra with their herds, between summer and winter pastures. Reindeer provide the Nenets with milk and meat, as well as fur and skins for clothing and shelter against the freezing environment. The Nenets are constantly on the move, searching for spongy plants called lichen that the reindeer can eat. They sleep in tents made of branches covered in reindeer skins.

INTERNET LINK

To take an interactive journey with the Nenets people and find out more about their way of life, go to **www.usborne-quicklinks.com**

Russian delicacies

Some foods in Russia have special significance. In everyday life, no meal is complete without bread, and when important people visit, they may be greeted with a gift of bread and salt. Certain festivals have foods associated with them, such as the Easter cheesecake called *pashka*. But one of Russia's most famous foods, and also one of the world's most expensive, is caviar. This delicacy is made from the eggs of sturgeon fish, which live mainly in the Caspian Sea.

Caviar from the Caspian Sea is sold in tiny tins like these. The cost of a single tin could feed a whole Russian family for up to a week.

Arts and crafts

Anton Chekhov wrote plays about Russian life around the start of the 20th century. One of his most famous is *The Seagull*.

Brave writers

Russian folk tales such as the *Firebird* and the *Snowmaiden* have been told for hundreds of years, to generations of children. But Russia's written literature first became famous worldwide in the 19th century, when writers published novels, plays and poetry to express their discontent with their country's politics. Some Russian writers got into trouble for their views, and suffered terrible punishments, such as exile to Siberia and death sentences.

World-famous ballet

Ballet came to Russia in the 18th century from France, and became a great art form there in the 19th and early 20th centuries. Choreographers worked with composers such as Tchaikovsky and Stravinsky to produce spectacular and ground-breaking performances. Two Russian ballet companies are now world-famous – the Kirov of St. Petersburg and the Bolshoi of Moscow. Young ballet dancers train hard from an early age in the hope of one day performing with them.

These Russian dolls fit inside each other. They are painted to look like girls dressed in peasant-style clothes.

Traditional crafts

Because Russia has huge areas of forest, many of its traditional crafts make use of wood. Some examples include painted religious icons and exquisitely carved toys. Lacquered wooden Easter eggs are traditional in Russia, and from this style developed dolls called *Matryoshka* – sets of hollow, differently sized wooden dolls that fit perfectly inside one another.

INTERNET LINK
For a link to a website where you can
read the story behind the *Nutcracker* ballet,
go to **www.usborne-quicklinks.com**

Chess in Russia

Vladimir Lenin, a former Russian leader, was an avid chess player. He encouraged all Russians to play this ancient Asian game, believing that it helped disciplined thought. Chess in Russia had traditionally been a game played only by the wealthy, but it quickly became widely popular. Schools were set up for excellent young players, and Russia has ever since been known for its high standard of chess.

Russian girls play chess at their school near Lake Baikal in southern Siberia.

In 2001, the Moscow Ballet performed a new version of the *Nutcracker*, featuring the Dove of Peace. This was to celebrate lasting peace between Russia and the USA, who were once enemies.

In Mongolia, men use golden eagles to help them hunt. Eagles are trained from a young age to catch prey such as rabbits, foxes, deer and wolves, which the hunters use for their skins. After ten years, the eagles are released into the wild, to breed.

Central Asia

Kazakhstan, Turkmenistan, Uzbekistan, Tajikistan,
Kyrgyzstan, Afghanistan, Mongolia

The dusty, windswept countries of Central Asia are bordered in the south and east by high, bleak mountain ranges – the Tien Shan, the Hindu Kush, the Pamirs and the Karakorum. Large areas of Kazakhstan and Turkmenistan are covered in open grassland, and much of Uzbekistan is hot desert, while Tajikistan, Kyrgyzstan and Afghanistan are crowded with towering, snowy peaks. All these countries, apart from Afghanistan, were once part of one enormous country known as the USSR, governed by Russia from Moscow.

Mongolia, to the east, shares similarities with these countries, although it is not always considered part of Central Asia. It too is covered in empty grasslands and deserts. Many of its people move around with their herds as they do in other Central Asian countries.

KAZAKHSTAN

Irtysh

Caspian Sea

Aral Sea

Lake Balkhash

UZBEKISTAN

TURKMENISTAN

Kara Kum Desert

KYRGYZSTAN

Tien Shan

Altai Mountains

MONGOLIA

Gobi Desert

Pamirs

Hindu Kush

TAJIKISTAN

AFGHANISTAN

0km   1,000km
0 miles   640 miles

Peaks and plains

Tajikistan's peaks

The eastern part of Tajikistan is sometimes called the roof of the
world because it is completely covered by the towering peaks of
the Pamirs, the world's second highest range of mountains.
So much of Tajikistan is mountainous that only around
one-tenth of its land is suitable for farming.

People can't survive for long on very
high mountains, but some do manage
to live on the lower mountain
slopes. As a result of its scenic
rocky landscape, Tajikistan
is one of the world's
poorest countries.

These mist-
swathed peaks are part
of the Pamir mountain range,
in northern Pakistan, near Tajikistan.

Mongolia is home to both
wild and tame horses. They
graze on its vast grasslands.

Grasslands of Asia

Much of central Asia is covered in dry grassland
called *steppe*. It stretches across Asia, from the
eastern edge of Europe to northern China, and
is the biggest area of grassland in the world.

There are few trees to give shade or shelter,
so it's hot on the *steppe* in summer, but bitterly
cold in winter. There's very little rain, and strong
winds whip across the flat landscape. Luckily, the
grasses have long, intertwined roots to anchor
themselves firmly in the ground against the
strong gusts. Common grassland animals include
rodents such as gerbils, mice and hamsters.
There are also herds of grazing animals such as
sheep, cattle and camels, belonging to farmers.

INTERNET LINK

For a link to a website where you can take
a virtual sightseeing trip in the Pamirs,
go to **www.usborne-quicklinks.com**

A man on camelback travels across the baked, arid landscape of the Kara Kum Desert in Turkmenistan.

Turkmenistan's desert

Turkmenistan is a spacious country, but few people live there, as it is mostly covered by the sandy wastes of the Kara Kum Desert. Its towns are built close to what little water there is, such as the man-made canal that runs through the desert. The desert is also dotted with places called oases where there's enough water for things to grow. The capital, Ashgabat, is built around an oasis in the south of the country.

As well as being dry, the Kara Kum Desert is also hot. Among the few kinds of animals that can survive such harsh conditions are spiders, scorpions and giant monitor lizards.

Jewel of Kyrgyzstan

One of Kyrgyzstan's most stunning natural features is Lake Issyk, a deep, clear lake nestled between ridges of the Tien Shan mountains, which form the country's border with China.

The lake is surrounded by towns and health resorts, as people believe that bathing in the lake's mineral-rich waters is good for them. The water is too salty for humans to drink or to use for watering the land nearby, but cattle are able to drink it. Many kinds of fish live in the lake, and it also provides a winter home for migrating water birds, because it never completely freezes over, even in deepest winter.

The dark patch below is Lake Issyk in Kyrgyzstan, between the high, snowy peaks of the Tien Shan mountain range. This photograph was taken from space by a satellite.

Harsh landscapes

Cotton is one of the crops grown in Afghanistan to be sold to other countries. These men are weighing cotton for sale at a market.

Russian rockets

The Baikonur Cosmodrome in Kazakhstan is the site of many of Russia's rocket launches. These provide money for both countries, as companies pay Russia to send satellites into orbit, and Russia pays Kazakhstan to use the land. There are serious drawbacks – used metal rocket parts rain down on Kazakhstan, and the toxic rocket chemicals affect the health of people living near Baikonur.

This rocket is on its way to the launch pad at the Baikonur Cosmodrome in Kazakhstan.

Cotton-growing countries

Kazakhstan, Uzbekistan, Turkmenistan, Kyrgyzstan and Tajikistan, which were once part of the USSR, contain vast stretches of flat land. The Moscow government used large areas of these countries to grow cotton, to be sold abroad. When they became independent in 1991, the countries were at last free to decide for themselves which crops to grow. Sadly, the years of intensive cotton farming had used up an enormous amount of precious river water and much of the land had become desert, unsuitable for new farms. Today there are still many cotton farms, which provide a useful source of income for the countries.

Aral Sea disaster

The Aral Sea has shrunk to one-third of its original size within the last fifty years, and could dry out completely during this century. This environmental disaster happened because water from the rivers that feed the lake was diverted for watering cotton crops. The Aral Sea's fishing and shipping industries have been ruined, and the air around it is now so dry and salty that it badly affects the health of many people living nearby.

A fishing boat stranded on dry land in Kazakhstan shows where the Aral Sea used to reach, before it began to dry up.

An Afghan family travels on the back of a donkey. Until recently, Afghan women were forced to cover their faces, as this woman has done.

INTERNET LINK

For a link to a website where you can see amazing photographs of fallen rockets and space junk from the Baikonur Cosmodrome, go to **www.usborne-quicklinks.com**

Nomadic herders

Many Central Asian people lead nomadic lives, which means they move regularly between different pastures with their herds of animals. The animals provide meat and milk as well as skins and wool for clothing and shelter. Nomadic people in Central Asia need to move around frequently, as much of the ground there is so dry that their animals quickly eat up all the available food.

Nomads get some of the extra things they need for themselves by trading with people living in the towns that they pass through on their travels. The townspeople need leather and meat, which the nomads supply in return for grain for their animals, cotton and silk thread, as well as metal and pottery objects such as knives and cooking pots.

23

Traditional life

On the sunny, windswept plains of Mongolia, a felt-covered tent like this provides shade and shelter.

Movable homes

Many families in central Asia live in movable tent-like homes, made of a wooden frame covered in warm felt panels. In some parts of Central Asia these are called *yurts*, and in Mongolia the felt tents are called *gers*. Some nomadic people move their tents regularly, following their herds to new pastures. But many now choose to stay in one place, such as Ulan Bator, the Mongolian capital city, where clusters of *gers* nestle in the shadows of apartment blocks.

Central Asian clothing

Most people living in cities in Central Asia wear western-style clothes, but many nomadic herders wear traditional costumes of long, loose tunics over baggy, striped trousers, made of woven cotton, silk or wool. These outfits allow room for movement and so are quite suitable for horseback riding, and both men and women wear them. People also wear warm, fluffy hats made of sheep's wool, to protect themselves from cold winds.

For special occasions, women and girls in Turkmenistan often put on silver headdresses like the one this girl is wearing.

Cities of Uzbekistan

A trade route which became known as the Silk Road once stretched across Asia. As well as silk, many other goods and ideas spread along the route. Buddhism reached China and Japan from India, while gunpowder and porcelain were introduced to Europe from China. The Silk Road passed through Uzbekistan, and its magnificent cities are filled with buildings covered in carvings and mosaics, constructed hundreds of years ago when the Silk Road was busiest.

Mongolian holy men

As in many other Asian countries, most people in Mongolia follow the Buddhist faith. Mongolia has its own particular kind of Buddhism with certain beliefs, ceremonies and features. For example, in Mongolia holy men called *lamas* make a living by providing people with advice about religious, medical or spiritual problems. *Lamas* also bless projects such as new buildings.

These boys attend a school where they will learn to be Buddhist holy men, or *lamas*, in Ulan Bator in Mongolia.

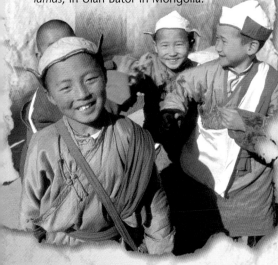

INTERNET LINK
For a link to a website where you can see how a *yurt* is built, go to
www.usborne-quicklinks.com

This dome covered in mosaic tiles tops one of the buildings in the Registan, the main central square of the ancient city of Samarqand, in Uzbekistan.

Riches and finery

Islamic architecture

Most people in Central Asia follow the religion of Islam, and their religious beliefs have influenced the style of architecture there. Buildings are often patterned with paintings and mosaics, but the decorations don't show people or animals, as some followers of Islam believe that humans should not create images of living things. For this reason, designs are made up of geometric shapes and plant-like patterns.

This is a detail from the ceiling of a mosque in Bukhara in Uzbekistan. It is made up of geometric patterns typical of Islamic places of worship.

Amazing carpets

For thousands of years, skilled craftworkers in Turkmenistan have produced exquisite carpets, made from the soft, silky wool of a sheep called the *Saryja*, which is unique to Turkmenistan. The carpets contain millions of individual knots, tied by hand. Carpets are traditionally traded at markets called *bazaars* in large cities and towns, along with camels, sheep and other goods. But these days, it's possible to buy carpets from Turkmenistan over the Internet, too.

Many symbols on carpets like this one from Turkmenistan represent different groups of people.

INTERNET LINK

For a link to a website where you can use your Central Asia knowledge to take part in a Mongolian horse race, go to **www.usborne-quicklinks.com**

Valuable horses

Horses are important in Central Asia to help people travel around, for their meat and for their milk, which can be made into a drink called *koumiss*. *Akhal-Teke* horses, a unique breed from Central Asia and Russia, are lean and light, with incredibly glossy coats. They can survive on very little food and water, but are still able to move extremely fast over long distances.

The sleek *Akhal-Teke* breed of horse is fast and agile. The horse shown here is black, but many *Akhal-Tekes* have shimmering golden coats.

A Mongolian *tsam* dancer's tall, elaborately carved mask has no eye holes, so the dancer inside must look out through the character's mouth.

Mongolian dances

Mongolian *tsam* dances are performed in Buddhist monasteries. The dances are religious rituals intended to pass on messages taken from Buddhist teachings to audiences. As part of their ceremony, *tsam* dances have dramatic songs, dance moves, music from gongs and trumpets as well as the highly decorated costumes of characters. These include animals, people, holy figures and devils, and they all have a range of personalities to help represent various positive and negative influences.

An Indian man rides an Asian elephant that has been hand-painted with decorative patterns for a festival.

The Indian Subcontinent

India, Pakistan, Nepal, Bhutan, Bangladesh, Sri Lanka, Maldives

The area known as the Indian Subcontinent is separated from the rest of Asia by the Himalaya and Hindu Kush mountain ranges. The climates of the countries in this region are affected by winds called monsoons, which give them a wet and a dry season each year.

Everyday life is strongly influenced by religion. Hinduism, Buddhism, Sikhism and Jainism all began in this region and still have many followers, and Islam and Christianity are also popular. There are followers of almost every religion in the world living in these countries today.

0km — 1,000km
0 miles — 640 miles

Hindu Kush

Indus

PAKISTAN

Himalayas

NEPAL

Ganges

BHUTAN

Tropic of Cancer

BANGLADESH

Arabian Sea

INDIA

Bay of Bengal

Andaman Islands (India)

Nicobar Islands (India)

SRI LANKA

MALDIVES

INDIAN OCEAN

Extreme landscapes

The Ganges

A tiny stream that emerges from a mountain spring on the slopes of the Himalayas eventually becomes a huge river called the Ganges. The Ganges flows across northeastern India and through Bangladesh, where it joins another huge river, the Brahmaputra. The main river then fragments into many smaller channels, forming a river delta that is the largest in the world.

Where the Ganges meets the sea, it passes the Sundarbans, a cluster of islands covered in swampy forests. The varied wildlife there includes the world's last few remaining Royal Bengal tigers.

INTERNET LINK

For a link to a website where you can take a snapshot tour of wildlife on the Indian Subcontinent, and try a Himalayan hiking game, go to **www.usborne-quicklinks.com**

This mysterious-looking photograph, taken from space, shows the River Ganges meeting the sea. The pale blue parts are the river channels of the Ganges flowing into the Indian Ocean, at the top of the picture. The dark blue parts show the land between the river channels.

Monsoon climate

Each year, seasonal winds called monsoons sweep across India and Bangladesh, lashing them with violent rainstorms or bringing dry, scorching weather. When the wind blows from the southwest, it passes over the Indian Ocean and brings heavy rain almost every day. But when the wind blows from the lands in the northeast, it brings no rain, so a dry season follows.

Farmers plant their crops to take advantage of the rainy season. However, if there is not enough rain one year, all the crops may fail. If there is too much rain, there may be devastating floods, and the crops are drowned.

The monsoon winds bring rain to Bangladesh's farmland every year, making it moist enough to grow crops on.

The Thar Desert

Along part of the border between India and Pakistan, the Thar Desert forms a vast expanse of dry sand and gravel. Strong winds shift the dunes, so the rolling landscape is always changing. There is no water in this desert at all, so people who live in the Thar must travel long distances out of the desert, on foot or by camel, to find it.

People in the Thar Desert use camels for travel, either riding them or using them to carry equipment. Camels can survive for days without water, and cope with desert sandstorms by sealing their nostrils shut.

The huge Himalayas

At the northern border of the Indian Subcontinent is the massive Himalaya mountain range. It formed around 55 million years ago, which is quite recent for a range of mountains.

The Earth's surface is made up of large pieces of rock called plates, which move incredibly slowly. This movement is what caused the Himalayas to form. Millions of years ago, India was separate from the Asian continent, but the Indian plate gradually drifted north, until it collided with the Asian plate. The land crumpled into the huge, rocky ridges that we call the Himalayas. The Indian plate is still moving north today, so the Himalayas continue to grow by a tiny amount every year.

A rare, clear view of Mount Everest, on the border between Nepal and China. The mountain is also known by its Tibetan name of Chomolangma, and its Nepalese name, Sagarmatha. It is the highest peak on Earth.

Warm, wet climates

Islands in danger

The Maldives are a group of over 1,000 tiny islands in the Indian Ocean. Many of them have sparkling white sandy beaches and lush groves of palm trees, and are popular travel destinations. The islands formed on coral reefs, made by the rocky skeletons of millions of tiny sea creatures. The Maldives are so low-lying that if the sea level ever rises they could be completely submerged. If the sea were also to become warmer, this could kill the coral, and the creatures and plants that live on it would die.

The green patches you can see are two of the Maldive islands. Coral reefs under the water show as light blue patches.

Each of these Sri Lankan fishermen is perching on a wooden stilt, while he uses a rod to catch fish from the shallow water.

Fishing in Sri Lanka

Sri Lanka is an island off the southern tip of India, surrounded by warm, shallow seas. One of its main industries is fishing. Many Sri Lankan fishermen use traditional methods: some fish from boats made of hollowed-out logs, others from perches on poles called stilts. Each stilt fisherman has his own stilt in a patch of shallow water. They usually fish in the cooler hours at sunrise and sunset, using long rods to catch the fish.

These women are picking tea in Sri Lanka. Each worker picks around twice her weight in tea leaves every day.

Tea plantations

Many hills in India and Sri Lanka are cloaked in bright green tea plants. Tea grows well in warm, moist climates like India's, but it prefers high ground, where mist and clouds protect it from the harshest sunlight. The world's biggest tea-producing region is hilly Assam, in northeast India. The tea plants grow in rows that seem to hug the shapes of the hills, and are kept pruned short to make it easier to pick their leaves. The leaves are dried out, rolled and packaged, to be sold all over the world.

Growing jute

The very wet, warm climate of Bangladesh and northeastern India is ideally suited for growing jute plants. These grow around 3m (10ft) high, and their long stems can be twisted together to make yarn. In the 18th century, jute was used to make ropes for ships. People then found they could weave it and began making it into sacks. These days, jute is used to make anything from woven mats to handbags.

As this man harvests jute plants in Bangladesh, he cuts the stems but leaves the roots behind to rot in the ground.

INTERNET LINK
For a link to a website with interactive, tea-related activities and facts, go to
www.usborne-quicklinks.com

Daily life

INTERNET LINK

For a link to a website about the small country of Bhutan, go to **www.usborne-quicklinks.com**

Setting her flower petals afloat on the River Ganges at Varanasi, this woman is making an offering to the Hindu gods.

India's city of pilgrims

All followers of the Hindu faith hope to make at least one religious journey, or pilgrimage, in their lifetime, to the city of Varanasi. During their visit, they bathe in the water of the River Ganges, which they believe to be sacred.

Steps called *ghats* line the riverbanks at Varanasi, leading down to the water's edge. Thousands of people crowd onto the *ghats*, especially at festival times, when they come to float lanterns and petals on the water, or to scatter the ashes of people who have died. Holy men called *sadhus* sit beside the river, ready to perform religious ceremonies for pilgrims visiting the city.

Schools in Pakistan

Most children in Pakistan go to public schools, that are free and open to everyone. But many of these schools are poor and can't provide desks, chairs or books. Private schools have much better facilities, but they're very expensive and few parents can afford them.

The other alternative is a religious school. Funded by religious groups, they are free to students, but open only to boys. Students study the *Qur'an*, the holy book of Islam, with other subjects such as mathematics and languages.

Like many public schools in Pakistan, this village school is very overcrowded. These children are studying in a classroom outside the walls of their school.

Bhutanese traditions

Bhutan is a tiny country in the Himalayas with a way of life quite untouched by modern ideas and technology. The capital city, Thimphu, is the only capital in the world with no traffic lights. Where busy roads meet, police direct the traffic from a hexagonal hut in the middle of the road. Thimphu is slowly expanding but new buildings are still built in traditional ways, from rocks, mud, bamboo and wood, decorated with painted patterns of flowers, animals and religious motifs.

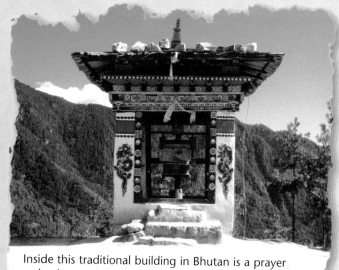

Inside this traditional building in Bhutan is a prayer wheel, containing written prayers. Followers of the Buddhist faith believe that spinning the wheel sends prayers out into the world.

Indian cooking

Curries are popular all over India, but there are different kinds and they vary depending on where they come from. Northern Indian curries are made with meat, fish or vegetables cooked with combinations of ground spices such as turmeric, cumin and coriander. They are usually served with flat bread. In southern India, most people tend to be vegetarian. Their curries are seasoned with fiery hot chilies, and usually served with rice.

These bright piles of powders are spices for sale at a market in northern India. They are to be used in cooking.

Place of many religions

Home of Hinduism

There are followers of many faiths in India, but the most popular religion there is Hinduism. Nearby Nepal also has a large Hindu following. Hinduism began in India over 4,000 years ago, making it one of the world's oldest religions. It is still thriving today, with millions of followers, and hundreds of festivals that happen throughout the Hindu year.

A Hindu holy man, or *sadhu*, wears this yellow mark, called a *tilak*, on his head to show that he is a member of a religious group.

Muslim memorial

The Taj Mahal, in India, is one of the world's most well-known Islamic buildings. Its walls and floors are inlaid with countless pieces of semi-precious stones and decorated with verses from the *Qur'an*. It was built by Emperor Shah Jahan in 1631, in memory of his wife, and took more than 20,000 men 22 years to build.

The Taj Mahal is made of white marble, and is reflected in a long pool. Its appearance is transformed throughout the day as light falls on it from different angles.

INTERNET LINK

For a link to a website with information on ancient India, its geography and religions, with stories to read and challenges to complete, go to
www.usborne-quicklinks.com

The origin of Sikhism

Sikhism was founded in the Punjab, a part of Pakistan and India where most people were once either Hindus or Muslims. Sikhism teaches that the truth of religion is the same, whatever a person's chosen faith, and that God sees everyone as equals. Today, Sikhs from all over the world make pilgrimages to the Golden Temple, in Amritsar in India. The temple is in the middle of a lake, which the city is named after: Amritsar means "pool of nectar".

Inside the Golden Temple in Amritsar, a priest reads from the *Adi Granth*, the Sikh holy scriptures.

Buddhist beginnings

Buddhism began near the border between present-day India and Nepal, over 2,500 years ago. Today, Buddhism is still popular in India and Nepal, but it has also spread to many other places in Asia, including China, Japan, Mongolia and many countries in Southeast Asia. Each region has its own style of Buddhism as well as different kinds of religious shrines and temples.

The flags tied to the top of this Buddhist shrine in Nepal have prayers written on them. Buddhists believe that when they flutter in the wind, the prayers are sent out around the world.

Poverty and progress

Indian independence

The countries we know today as India, Bangladesh and Pakistan were once ruled by the British. But the Indian people wanted independence, so during the early 20th century, Mahatma Gandhi led them in a peaceful resistance against British rule.

In 1947, the British granted India independence. The land was divided into Hindu-dominated India and a homeland for Muslims called Pakistan. Many people died in riots as millions of Hindus and Muslims crossed the borders between them. In 1971, East Pakistan became a separate Muslim country called Bangladesh.

Mahatma Gandhi led India's struggle for independence. He dressed in a simple loincloth and shawl to identify with India's poorest people.

The small country of Bangladesh is overpopulated and most of its people are extremely poor. These children live in crowded slums in Dhaka, the capital city.

Bangladesh in poverty

Bangladesh is one of the world's most crowded countries, and one of the poorest. Most people there work for a tiny wage and own no land. If the harvest is bad one year and people need to buy extra food for their families, they can borrow money from their rich, land-owning employers. But this means they are bound to keep working for their employers to pay off their debts.

INTERNET LINK
To find out more about the people and culture of India and Bangladesh, go to
www.usborne-quicklinks.com

38

This man is painting a billboard in Mumbai, for *Devdas*, the most expensive and successful Indian movie of all time.

Movies from India

India produces more movies every year than any other country. Many of these are made in the studios of Mumbai, nicknamed "Bollywood" (after its old name of Bombay). Bollywood movies are usually busy and loud, with song and dance routines to tell the story, which is often romantic or dramatic.

Modern India

After India gained independence in 1947, Jawaharlal Nehru, the new prime minister, began to modernize his country. He organized the building of new factories, as well as a system of roads and railways to connect them. Partly as a result of Nehru's reforms, in only a few decades, India has become a world leader in science and technology. Many millions of people in India work in the IT industry, or as scientists helping to develop new products such as medicines.

39

The Great Wall of China winds all the
way across northern China. The wall
was built gradually, starting over 2,000
years ago, to protect China from
invaders from the north.

Eastern Asia

China, Japan, North Korea, South Korea, Taiwan

The biggest country in Eastern Asia is China, and more people live there than in any other country in the world. China's far north is covered in low deserts and grasslands, but in the west, a vast area of highlands forms the Plateau of Tibet, which is overshadowed only by the Himalayas, the highest mountains in the world. In eastern China there are large areas of farmland watered by wide rivers, and just off the coast is the rugged, beautiful island of Taiwan. Above Taiwan, the steep, forest-clad mountains of the Korean Peninsula jut out into the East China Sea. To the far east, the country of Japan is made up of a long chain of volcanic islands. The majority of its people live clustered close to the coasts.

0km   1,000km
0 miles   640 miles

Hokkaido

NORTH KOREA

Sea of Japan

JAPAN

Gobi Desert

SOUTH KOREA

Honshu

Kunlun Mountains

CHINA

Huang He (Yellow)

East China Sea

Plateau of Tibet

Chang Jiang (Yangtze)

Himalayas

TAIWAN

Tropic of Cancer

Hainan

Threatened environments

The Yangtze

The River Yangtze snakes across the huge country of China, from the high Plateau of Tibet in the west to the city of Shanghai on the eastern coast. It is the longest river in Asia and the third longest river in the world. The Yangtze provides a vital travel link between many of China's cities, and each day hundreds of thousands of ships transport people and goods along it.

An enormous concrete dam has been built across the Yangtze, to generate electricity for millions of homes, control flooding and allow ships to reach even more cities upriver. However, many people all over the world are opposed to the dam, and think it will damage the environment.

The River Yangtze flows through several gorges lined with steep, rocky cliffs. This ship is entering the Xiling Gorge.

These built-up areas, close to Mount Fuji in Japan, could be in danger if the volcano erupts in the future.

Mount Fuji

On a clear day, the snowy slopes of Mount Fuji are visible from Tokyo, Japan's capital city. Its beautiful, almost-symmetrical cone makes Mount Fuji one of the most famous volcanoes in the world. It is also the highest mountain in Japan, and thousands of adventurous people climb it every day, scrambling up the slopes through the night to reach the peak in time for sunrise.

Although the Japanese used to worship Mount Fuji, believing it to be home to a goddess, the volcano is now a potential threat to millions of homes. It last erupted around 300 years ago, and scientists believe that it could erupt again in the future, with disastrous results for the cities and towns nearby.

INTERNET LINK

For a link to a website where you can find out about the building of the Three Gorges Dam across the River Yangtze, go to **www.usborne-quicklinks.com**

Central China is home to
endangered giant pandas.
Their woodland homes can
be destroyed when people cut
down trees to clear farmland.

China's forests

The last giant pandas left in the
wild live in the mist-shrouded
mountain forests of central China.
There are now only around 1,000 of
these black-and-white bears left. Giant
pandas eat the tender shoots of a kind
of grass called bamboo, and they spend
up to 16 hours every day searching for
enough to eat. They are endangered
because bamboo has been cut down in
China to make space for farming.

China's desert

The Taklimakan Desert, in northwest
China, is the second biggest sandy
desert in the world. Conditions there
are so harsh that many people have
died trying to cross it. In the day, it is
baking hot, but at night it is freezing
cold. There are often sandstorms,
and many deadly snakes live
there. Millions of years ago,
the Taklimakan Desert was
a sea, and it is possible to find
chunks of ancient coral there,
among the rocks.

The mounds you can see either side of
this man are the tops of buildings that
were buried many years ago by the
sands of the Taklimakan Desert.

43

Useful land

Industry in Taiwan

Many of Taiwan's factories produce plastics and dyes to be sold to other countries.

The island of Taiwan is remarkably pretty, with steep peaks towering over leafy forests. The country is too small to grow many crops or to have its own abundant natural resources, but it is known worldwide as a place for manufacturing and trade. All kinds of electronic and other goods are made there to be sold to other countries around the globe.

Crops in China

The River Yangtze roughly divides China's north and south. The main food crop in the cooler, drier north is wheat, which is made into noodles or boiled with water to make porridge. In southern China, the main food crop is rice. The warm, moist climate is ideal for rice, and when big rivers such as the Yangtze flood each year, they provide huge areas of rich farmland where it can grow. China produces more rice than any other country in the world, but most of this is used to feed southern China's growing population – hardly any is sold to other countries.

Rice fields need plenty of attention, but as hundreds of millions of people live in southern China, a supply of farm workers there is not a problem. These workers are planting young rice plants.

INTERNET LINK

For a link to a website about rice, Asia's most important food crop, with facts, figures and a description of life in a rice-growing family, go to **www.usborne-quicklinks.com**

River fishing

In parts of China and Japan, some river fishermen use birds called cormorants to help them catch fish. Each fisherman has several birds tied to his boat with twine. The twine is fastened to rings around the birds' necks, tight enough to keep them from swallowing fish. On a signal from the fishermen, the birds dive into the water and catch fish in their beaks, then bring them back to the boat. When fishing is over for the night, the rings are removed and the cormorants can eat.

A cormorant has dived underwater and managed to catch hold of this slippery fish in its beak.

Japanese springs

Japan has around 100 active volcanoes, and is also prone to earthquakes. But there are some benefits to living in such a volcanic region. All over Japan, there are hot springs, where volcanic activity heats the water and makes it pleasantly warm for bathing. People visit these hot springs, but they're not the only ones. Monkeys called snow macaques have discovered that the warm pools are good places to escape the freezing temperatures of Japan's bitterly cold winters.

This animal is a snow macaque. It is taking a dip in a volcanic hot pool, to warm itself up in the freezing cold of a Japanese winter.

45

Far Eastern style

Chinese cooking

Different parts of China have their own unique cooking styles. In southern areas, food is steamed in bamboo baskets and delicately seasoned. In the west, many dishes are spiced with hot chilies and pepper. Meat and vegetable dishes are usually served with rice in the south, but with noodles in the north. Lavish meals for special occasions are made up of a selection of dishes, picked to provide contrasting tastes, smells and textures.

This small dish of soy sauce is for dipping food in.

A Chinese meal often has several dishes served with rice or noodles. People help themselves, using chopsticks to pick up small pieces of food to eat with their rice or noodles.

INTERNET LINK

For a link to a website with information on life in Japan and recipes you can try, go to **www.usborne-quicklinks.com**

Japanese homes

Many Japanese homes are built of wood and decorated simply, using natural materials. The floor is covered in thick *tatami* mats woven from straw. People sit on cushions on the floor, and sleep there too, on *futon* mattresses that are rolled up out of the way in the day. Sliding wood-and-paper *shoji* screens create separate rooms.

Light filters through paper screens into the dining room of this Japanese home.

Busy Chinese city

Hong Kong, in China, is one of the world's most crowded and exciting cities. It is squeezed onto an island, and land there is scarce and expensive. People live crammed into small apartments in high-rise blocks, and the skyline bristles with tall office skyscrapers. Many people choose to live on the nearby mainland or other islands, where there is more space.

In Hong Kong, in China, apartments, stores and offices crowd closely together.

Japanese clothes

Most Japanese people wear western-style clothes such as jeans, skirts and t-shirts. But for parties, weddings, visits to shrines and other special occasions, they often wear *kimonos*. A *kimono* is a wrap-around gown with flowing sleeves, fastened at the waist with a wide belt called an *obi*. Men, women and children all wear *kimonos*. Some *kimonos* are made of embroidered silk and are extremely valuable, but they can also be made of cheap, printed cotton. The style depends on who is wearing the *kimono*, what the occasion is and also on the time of year.

This girl is wearing a *kimono* for the Shichigosan festival, a Japanese celebration for girls aged 3 and 7, and boys aged 3 and 5.

Religions

Chinese New Year

The highlight of the Chinese calendar is the New Year festival. Families remember their ancestors with a feast on New Year's Eve. On New Year's Day, they eat vegetarian food, as the Chinese believe this will bring them a long, happy life. Around this time, people also light scented bamboo incense sticks and pray to their ancestors. The celebrations last for 15 days, building up to the Lantern Festival on the final night, when there are spectacular lantern displays and parades of people in fantastic costumes.

During the Andong Mask Dance Festival, people pay their respects to spirits by performing dances wearing masks like these.

Korean festivals

Some of Korea's many festivals are a chance for people to remember the ancient spirit world. Others are based on the teachings of Confucius, who encouraged people to worship their ancestors. Korean life is closely linked to farming, and so many of the festivals there are based on the seasons of the year and the harvest. But now, most South Koreans are Christian and celebrate Christmas and Easter, too.

A dancer holds up a spectacular dragon's head. He's taking part in a Dragon Dance, in Hong Kong, as part of the Chinese New Year celebrations.

INTERNET LINK

For a link to a website where you can learn more about the Chinese New Year festival, go to **www.usborne-quicklinks.com**

48

The Japanese spirit world

The Shinto religion is unique to Japan. Its followers believe that spirits called *kami* live in natural things, such as wind, mountains, rivers and trees. Shinto shrines are simple, peaceful places, often in a forest or by water, where people can be close to nature. At the entrance to a shrine is a gate called a *torii*, symbolizing the border between the human and the spirit worlds. Inside, people pray and make offerings to keep evil spirits away.

For followers of Shinto, these red pillars form gates that symbolize entry to the spirit world. The inscriptions are the names of the people who gave money for each gate.

Tibetan Buddhism

Tibet was once an independent country, with its own religion, a branch of Buddhism called *Vajrayana*. In 1950, Tibet became part of China. Religion was discouraged for many years, but now, Buddhism is once again a very visible part of life in Tibet, and monasteries that were closed have been re-opened. Many young boys spend some time in the monasteries, living as trainee monks called novices as part of their general education.

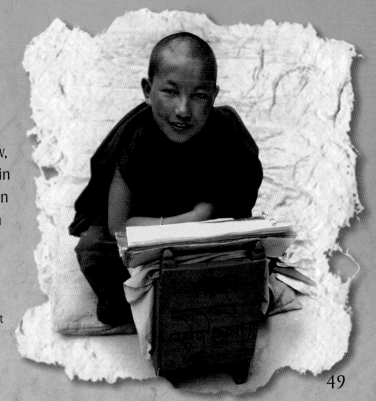

This boy is studying to be a monk at a Tibetan Buddhist monastery in Lhasa, Tibet's main city. Young monks study the Tibetan language and Buddhist teachings.

49

Art and entertainment

Japan's national sport

A Japanese *sumo* wrestler warms up before a fight. Behind him sit his opponent and the referee.

The traditional national sport of Japan is *sumo*, a form of wrestling, watched by millions at live matches or on TV. Two wrestlers called *rikishi* fight each other in a small ring. Each tries to push his opponent out of the ring, or force him to touch the floor with any part of the body apart from his feet. Most matches only last for a few seconds. *Rikishi* are highly respected in Japan, and wear special costumes even when they are not fighting, so that everyone can see they are *sumo* wrestlers.

Chinese opera

Opera has always been popular in China and Taiwan, and in the past it's even been used to send out political messages as well as to tell stories. Each performance is an entertaining blend of mime, dance, singing and swordfighting. The props used on stage are quite simple, such as an oar to show a boat, or a strip of ribbon to represent a river. Performances are accompanied by a small band of string and percussion players.

The mainly red costume of this Beijing Opera performer tells the audience that he is playing a loyal character.

This Chinese Buddhist monk is learning *kung fu* at Shaolin Temple, a place famous for the study of *kung fu*.

Martial arts

Martial arts are often regarded as sports but in fact they began as philosophies or ways of thinking, in Eastern Asia. Martial arts students learn skills of mind and body that they can use to defend themselves. Well-known martial arts include *judo* from Japan, *tae kwon do* from Korea and *kung fu* from China.

Kung fu began thousands of years ago, in central China. It uses kicking and punching techniques, and was made famous around the world in the 20th century by Bruce Lee, a movie star from Hong Kong.

Chinese calligraphy

Chinese calligraphy, or the art of writing, is based on the written Chinese language, and has also been adapted for the Japanese and Korean written languages. Written Chinese has thousands of characters, each of which is a symbol, formed by an intricate pattern of strokes, drawn in a particular order. Calligraphy is traditionally drawn using a brush and ink, and there are many different calligraphic styles, varying from spiky, separated and angular, to free-flowing and joined-up.

Chinese calligraphy is written from top to bottom, and from right to left. Water is added to a solid ink-block to make a pool of ink that the brush is dipped into.

INTERNET LINK

For a link to a website with an introduction to Japanese calligraphy, and a chance to try virtual calligraphy, go to **www.usborne-quicklinks.com**

A gigantic statue of the Buddha (the founder of Buddhism) provides a place for a young Buddhist monk to sit in a park in Laos.

52

Mainland Southeast Asia

Burma (Myanmar), Thailand, Laos, Vietnam, Cambodia

In this book, Southeast Asia has been divided into Mainland Southeast Asia and Maritime Southeast Asia, which you can read about in the next section. Mainland Southeast Asia is made up of five countries that fit together, jigsaw-like, on a knob of land that juts out from the southeastern corner of Asia. The River Mekong flows through them all and forms natural borders between Laos and the countries of Burma (Myanmar) and Thailand.

All the countries share similar climates, with gently sloping landscapes covered in tropical forests and good farmland. Most people in these countries are followers of Buddhism, and it is usual to see Buddhist monks wandering the streets in their golden, saffron-dyed robes, and to spot the steeply sloping roofs of Buddhist temples poking up above the dark green foliage of the trees.

0km   1,000km
0 miles   640 miles

Tropic of Cancer

Irrawaddy

BURMA (MYANMAR)

LAOS

South China Sea

Bay of Bengal

Mekong

THAILAND

Andaman Sea

CAMBODIA

VIETNAM

Gulf of Thailand

Waterways and plantations

Linking countries

The River Mekong, which flows from China through Burma (Myanmar), Thailand, Laos, Cambodia and Vietnam, is the longest river in Southeast Asia. Boats can travel along much of the river's length, apart from a dangerous section in Cambodia near the Khone Falls.

The Mekong helps link the countries of Mainland Southeast Asia. Many of the 60 million people who live near the river are in small villages that can only be reached by boat. The countries in this region transport goods along the Mekong to trade with each other. They also use the river to transport goods to ports on the South China Sea, from where they can be traded with countries all over the world.

Cambodia's big lake

A net stretched between boats across a river helps these men catch fish swimming away from the shrinking Tonle Sap Lake in Cambodia.

The Tonle Sap, in Cambodia, is the biggest lake in Southeast Asia. It is connected to the large Mekong river by a much smaller river. In the dry season, the lake is shallow enough for a person to stand up in. But during the rainy season, it's over ten times deeper. This happens because the small river's flow changes direction twice each year. During the rainy season, the Mekong's floodwaters force water back up the small river into the lake, but in the dry season the river flows the other way, and the lake's waters sink again.

Here you can see part of the River Mekong flowing through Laos. It's the rainy season, and the river is very full of sediment washed from the land, which makes it look pinkish-brown.

Thousands of small, limestone islands like these are scattered across the still waters of Halong Bay, in northern Vietnam.

Vietnam's dragon

Southeast Asia has some incredibly dramatic coastlines. Halong Bay, in Vietnam, curves around the northwestern corner of the South China Sea. It is studded with over 3,000 small islands jutting out of the calm waters.

The islands form fantastic shapes, and their silhouettes inspire names such as Dragon Island and Man's Head Island. Some are hollow, their insides carved out by sea water to form caves. A Vietnamese legend tells that Halong Bay and its many scattered islands were formed when a giant dragon landed, and swished its massive tail from side to side in the sea.

INTERNET LINK

For a link to a website where you can take a photographic tour of the River Mekong region in the south of Vietnam, go to **www.usborne-quicklinks.com**

Coconuts in Thailand

In the wild, the seeds from coconut palms drift on the sea to places where new plants can take root. This is why the beaches in many hot countries are fringed by coconut palms. But products from coconut palms are very useful, and so many farmers in hot countries such as Thailand cultivate large crops of them in plantations. Coconuts can be eaten raw, and are also used in cooking. Even the hairy outer husks are used to make brushes and sacks.

These men are removing the outer husks from freshly picked coconuts, on the island of Koh Samui in southern Thailand. Each coconut palm can produce up to 100 coconuts every year.

55

Hard workers

Gold from the Mekong

Many Buddhist temples in Southeast Asia are adorned with gold decorations and statues coated in paper-thin gold leaf. People rub gold leaf onto parts of temples or statues of the Buddha (the founder of Buddhism) as a sign of respect.

People search in the River Mekong for gold to sell. There is gold in the mud and rocks of the riverbed, which is stirred up by the flowing water. People use wooden pans to pick through the mud for flecks and nuggets of gold. The money they earn can help them buy expensive items such as farm equipment.

There are small amounts of gold in the muddy Mekong riverbed. This woman from Laos is trying to sift out specks of gold using a shallow pan.

Working elephants

Southeast Asia is home to thousands of Asian elephants. In Thailand, most are trained to work, either hauling logs from felled trees or carrying tourists on treks. Each working elephant has its own keeper, who trains and feeds it.

As forests are cut down in Thailand, the areas where elephants can live shrink. Many keepers bring their elephants to cities such as Bangkok to work, but it's hard to find enough food for their elephants there.

This young working elephant is being washed by its trainer at an elephant hospital in Thailand.

Fishing on Lake Inle

A fisherman stands on the back of his boat on Lake Inle. From here, he can easily see fish swimming in the lake's waters.

Lake Inle, in Burma (Myanmar), is home to the Intha people. They use a unique method called leg-rowing to get around the lake on their boats. A fisherman stands at the back of his narrow, flat boat on one leg, and wraps the other leg around his long oar, pushing back with his calf to propel the boat forward. This leaves one hand free for him to move the conical bamboo trap into position to net fish.

When the fisherman becomes tired, he can switch to rowing with his other leg.

INTERNET LINK

For a link to a website with a visual introduction to the difficulties faced by the people of Burma (Myanmar), go to **www.usborne-quicklinks.com**

Water buffaloes

Many farmers in Southeast Asia use water buffaloes to work on rice fields and move heavy logs. Buffaloes cope with the hot climate by taking frequent dips in rivers or swamps to coat themselves in mud, which protects them from the burning sun and biting insects. But the buffaloes' role is threatened by modern farm machinery. Unlike buffaloes, machinery doesn't need a break during the hottest part of the day.

Two water buffaloes pull a farm cart in the hills of Thailand. Asian farmers have used buffaloes for over 2,000 years, and the animals are very precious to them. The buffaloes sleep near the house, guarded by the family dogs.

Village and city life

Mountain people

In the past, many people journeyed from China and Tibet to settle in the hills of Southeast Asia. Today, descendants of these people still live in the northern hills of Thailand, Vietnam, Burma (Myanmar) and Laos, as well as southern China. The groups all have different spoken languages, traditions, religions and styles of clothing. Many tourists visit their villages to see their ways of life. Some people think this threatens the villagers and treats them unfairly, but others argue that it brings money to the communities.

This Padaung woman lives in Thailand. For most of her life she has worn brass rings around her neck, which push her shoulders down, making her neck look longer.

Working villages

In many villages in Southeast Asia, all the villagers concentrate on making one particular product. This means they can produce large quantities of things to sell, such as carved wooden furniture, paper umbrellas or incense sticks – short slivers of perfumed bamboo designed to be burned slowly. Millions of incense sticks are used in the region every day for religious ceremonies, so they are always in demand. A single incense factory worker can make up to 15,000 sticks in one day.

This Vietnamese girl makes incense sticks by rolling strips of bamboo in fine sawdust. She adds perfume, then leaves the sticks to dry.

Bustling Bangkok

Bangkok, the capital city of Thailand, is one of the biggest and busiest cities in Southeast Asia. It is built on the banks of the Chao Phraya river, and is criss-crossed with a network of canals, called *khlongs*, which are teeming with small boats. The wide city streets seethe with traffic jams and the hot, damp air is thick with exhaust fumes.

But Bangkok is also famous for its glittering golden spires, richly ornamented palaces and secluded temples. A famous, old temple in Bangkok is Wat Pho, home of one of the largest Buddha images in Thailand.

This huge golden statue of the Buddha is in one of Bangkok's temples, Wat Pho. The soles of the feet are inlaid with mother-of-pearl designs, including 108 pictures of the Buddha at different stages of his life.

INTERNET LINK

For a link to a website where you can see stunning photographs of some of Bangkok's many temples, go to **www.usborne-quicklinks.com**

Incredible temples

Cambodian temple

The towers of Angkor Wat, in Cambodia, represent the peaks of Mount Meru, home of the Hindu gods.

Angkor Wat is a huge temple in the ruined city of Angkor, once the capital of the Khmer kingdom in present-day Cambodia. It was built over 1,000 years ago, and has both Hindu and Buddhist features. Many carvings on its walls tell stories from Hindu mythology.

Thailand invaded Angkor repeatedly, and so the Khmers moved their capital city, leaving Angkor to become overgrown by jungle. But the French brought the city to the attention of the outside world again, in 1860. Angkor Wat's ruins were restored, and now, thousands of tourists visit them every year.

Thailand's ruined capital

The city of Ayutthaya was once the capital city of Thailand. During that time, over 400 Buddhist monasteries were built there. In 1767, Ayutthaya was ransacked by the Burmese, and its public buildings were badly burned, along with many family homes.

The city was abandoned, and Thailand's capital was moved south to Bangkok. A collection of crumbling brick temples with towers called *stupas* and various statues of the Buddha are all that remain of the old city of Ayutthaya today.

INTERNET LINK

For a link to a website where you can explore the ancient city of Angkor with amazing virtual reality panoramas, go to **www.usborne-quicklinks.com**

This is the Wat Phra Sri Samphet, one of many ruined temples in the ancient city of Ayutthaya, in central Thailand.

Cambodian dancers wear ornate gold and silk costumes. The designs have hardly changed for hundreds of years.

Temple dancers

Traditional Cambodian dances are performed in temples, and often tell religious stories. The dancers are beautiful young girls, who represent *apsaras*, or heavenly beings. Their moves are flowing and graceful and the dancers wear tranquil smiles. Originally, the dances were performed for royalty and monks.

Famous golden rock

One of the most sacred Buddhist sites in Burma (Myanmar) is Kyaiktiyo Paya, the Golden Rock Pagoda. Most Burmese people try to visit it at least once in their lifetime. The pagoda is perched on top of a huge rock coated with gold leaf, precariously balanced on the edge of a cliff. People believe there is one of the Buddha's hairs inside the pagoda, and that this keeps the boulder from tumbling down the mountainside. Sometimes the rock sways, but it never quite falls.

Devoted visitors to Kyaiktiyo Paya in Burma (Myanmar) crowd close to the golden rock. Only men are allowed to touch it.

61

The lush, green landscape on the island of Luzon in the Philippines is typical of Southeast Asia. Terraced paddy fields have been cut into the hillside and planted with tender rice shoots.

Maritime Southeast Asia

Malaysia, Singapore, Indonesia, Brunei, Philippines, East Timor

Maritime means "near the sea". The lower part of Southeast Asia is sometimes given this name because it is made up of over 24,000 islands and much of its land is close to the sea. Indonesia alone has over 17,000 islands, stretching from Sumatra in the west, as far as New Guinea in the east. Only the western part of the island of New Guinea belongs to the Asian country of Indonesia; the island is usually considered part of Oceania.

The long coastlines of Maritime Southeast Asia are lapped by tropical seas. Most of this area is hot and the air is extremely damp, except for a few of Indonesia's rockier islands, which are quite dry. Many of the islands are covered in rainforest and the larger ones are mountainous. Indonesia also has hundreds of volcanoes, many of which are active.

Wild living

Volcanoes of Indonesia

Indonesia has more active volcanoes than any other country in the world, running along the length of its main islands. The most active volcano in Indonesia today is Merapi, on the island of Java. But the largest volcanic eruption in recorded history may have been when Tambora erupted on the island of Sumbawa, in 1815. Ash fell on many Indonesian islands up to 1,300km (800 miles) away, and blocked out the Sun's light, causing unusually cold weather around the world.

The cone-shaped mounds you can see here are active and extinct volcanoes in Indonesia. The steaming crater on the left is Mount Bromo.

Rainforest wildlife

Tropical forests cover large areas of Indonesia and are home to a variety of rare animal species, including Sumatran tigers, long-snouted Malayan tapirs and large apes, such as long-armed silvery gibbons.

Many apes hardly ever come down to the ground. Instead, they use their strong limbs to swing through the branches of trees. The apes that live in the wild in Southeast Asia are becoming endangered as trees are cut down in the forests where they live. But some of the areas are now protected national parks.

This young orangutan is hanging in a tree in Tanjung Puting National Park on Sumatra, a large Indonesian island.

INTERNET LINK

For a link to a website about the terrifying waves that can occur as a result of earthquakes and volcanic eruptions, go to **www.usborne-quicklinks.com**

The swirling cloud above is a storm called a typhoon approaching the islands of the Philippines (shown with outlines) in April 2003.

Isolated island creatures

Many of Southeast Asia's islands are havens for rare creatures that don't exist in the wild in other parts of the world. The hot, rocky island of Komodo, in Indonesia, is home to the world's largest lizard, the Komodo dragon. Groups of dragons also live on the nearby islands of Rinca, Padar and Flores, but it is still considered to be an endangered species. This is because the dragons live in a relatively small area of the world, and a single natural disaster such as a volcanic eruption could wipe out every single one.

Stormy Philippines

The mountainous islands of the Philippines take the full, frightening force of tropical storms called typhoons, that sweep in from the Pacific Ocean to the east. Around 20 typhoons hit the Philippines every year, lashing the islands with torrential rain, and winds strong enough to blow people off their feet. People are killed by typhoons in the Philippines each year, and they also cause terrible wind damage, flattening buildings and crops. The heavy rains cause water levels to rise suddenly, and there are often devastating flash floods and mudslides. Even after a storm has passed, there are dangers from damaged electricity cables and diseases spread by a lack of fresh water.

A bite from a Komodo dragon like this one can seriously injure a person. The mouths of these giant lizards contain deadly germs.

Farming and environment

Rice terraces

Rice is Asia's main food, so it is grown in many Asian countries with climates that are warm, wet and sunny enough. The steamy, tropical climates of the Philippines and Indonesia are ideal for growing rice, but much of the farmland in these countries is extremely hilly. So they can grow rice on the hillsides, farmers dig out flat terraces in the land. These keep the water the rice needs from washing away. Other hill farmers grow rice dry, which means it doesn't need to stand in water.

Rice grows on terraced farmland in Indonesia. The plants stand in a layer of water, which helps them grow and makes it easier for the farmers to control weeds.

Sugar cane

A man collects sugar cane to take to a factory, where it will be turned into sugar.

Sugar cane is a very useful crop that grows in Indonesia and the Philippines, as well as other tropical countries around the world. It's a type of giant grass, almost all of which can be used for food. The stems are squeezed to drain the juice out and then boiled, to leave grains of sugar. Any pulpy leftovers are used to make animal feed. Liquid from the pressed sugar cane also makes a sweet, refreshing drink.

Cash crops

Much of Southeast Asia's land is used to grow crops that don't feed the local population, but are turned into products that can be sold to other countries. These are sometimes called cash crops. Cash crops that grow in this region include sugar cane, rubber, and spices such as pepper.

Rubber trees grow extremely well in the warm, moist climates of Indonesia and Malaysia, and many farmers there plant them in closely-spaced rows. Rubber is made from a liquid called latex that gathers beneath the bark of the tree. Farmers cut sloping grooves in the bark of the rubber trees and collect the latex that trickles out.

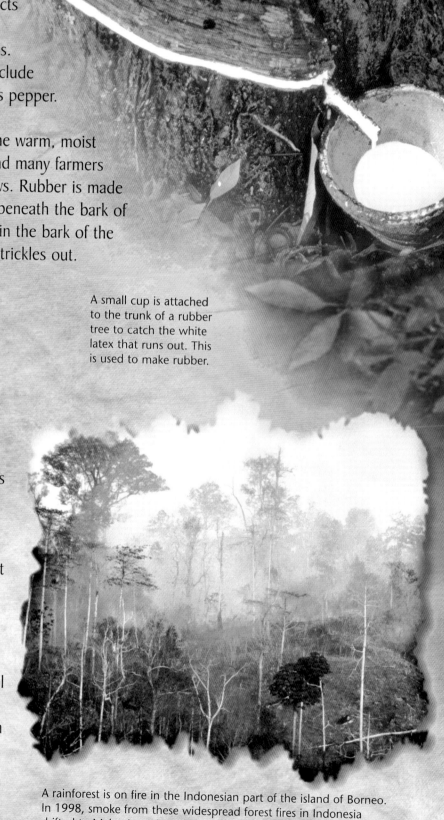

A small cup is attached to the trunk of a rubber tree to catch the white latex that runs out. This is used to make rubber.

INTERNET LINK

For a link to a website where you can explore Borneo's rainforest at night and discover the animals that live there, go to **www.usborne-quicklinks.com**

Forests in danger

Southeast Asia's lush rainforests are threatened by the cutting down of trees for commercial logging and to make space for farming. There are also massive forest fires. Some fires happen naturally and actually help certain forest plants to reproduce. But people also start fires to clear large areas of forest quickly. During very dry seasons, these small, man-made fires can spread rapidly, resulting in huge, out-of-control blazes that destroy millions of trees, plants and forest creatures. Smoke from the very big fires can drift and cause dangerously poor air quality in cities far away. This can affect people's health and even make plane travel hazardous.

A rainforest is on fire in the Indonesian part of the island of Borneo. In 1998, smoke from these widespread forest fires in Indonesia drifted to Malaysia and caused terrible air pollution there.

Spiritual beliefs

Old and new religions

Today, the majority of people living in the Philippines and East Timor are Christians. But before European settlers introduced Christianity to the region around 450 years ago, the main religion there was ancestor worship. Now, many people perform traditional ancestor worship alongside Christianity and other world religions such as Islam and Buddhism.

This girl is preparing for a Philippine festival called *Dinagyang*, which celebrates the arrival of Christianity with loud music, bright costumes and dancing.

Influence of Islam

Indonesia, Malaysia and Brunei together contain more followers of Islam, or Muslims, than any other region in the world. There are also many Muslims living in Singapore and the Philippines, and as a result there are mosques all over this region. Mosques have distinctive rounded domes and towers called minarets, from which Muslims are called to prayer. Many non-religious buildings in this region have also been influenced by aspects of Islamic architecture.

The Ubudiah Mosque is one of the most famous mosques in Malaysia. The towers each have space at the top for a man called a *muezzin* to call Muslims to prayer.

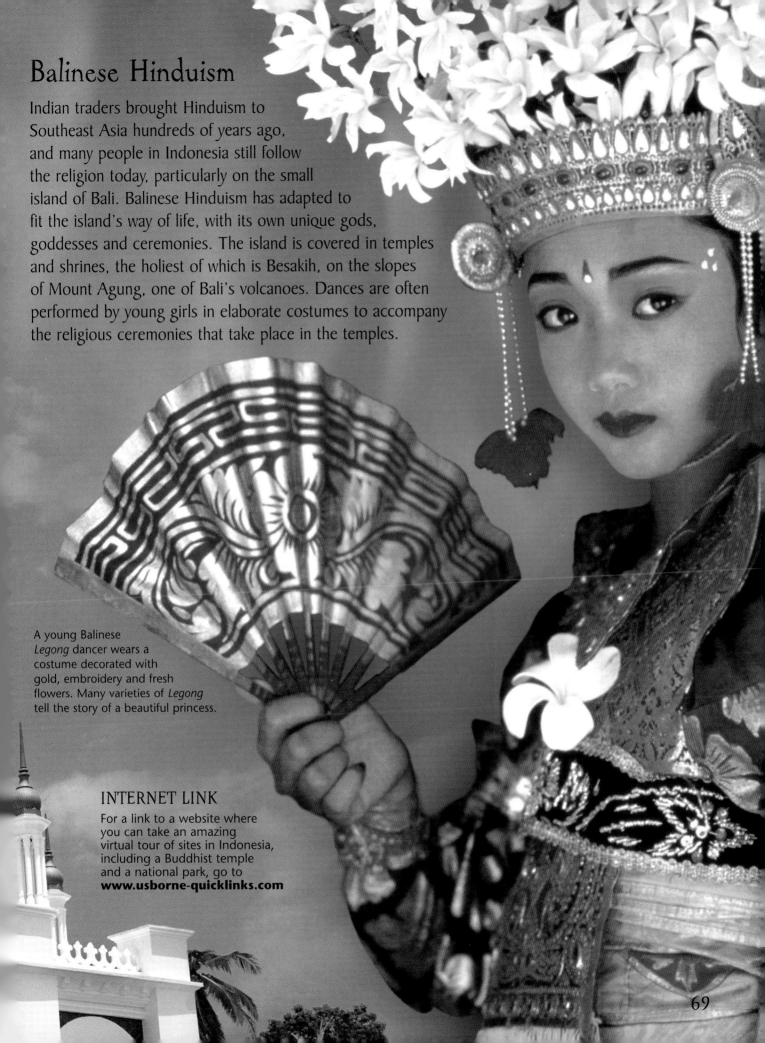

Balinese Hinduism

Indian traders brought Hinduism to Southeast Asia hundreds of years ago, and many people in Indonesia still follow the religion today, particularly on the small island of Bali. Balinese Hinduism has adapted to fit the island's way of life, with its own unique gods, goddesses and ceremonies. The island is covered in temples and shrines, the holiest of which is Besakih, on the slopes of Mount Agung, one of Bali's volcanoes. Dances are often performed by young girls in elaborate costumes to accompany the religious ceremonies that take place in the temples.

A young Balinese *Legong* dancer wears a costume decorated with gold, embroidery and fresh flowers. Many varieties of *Legong* tell the story of a beautiful princess.

INTERNET LINK

For a link to a website where you can take an amazing virtual tour of sites in Indonesia, including a Buddhist temple and a national park, go to **www.usborne-quicklinks.com**

Old and new traditions

Dyed Indonesian cloth

Batik is the name for the Indonesian technique of dyeing patterned cloth using wax. To make *batik*, melted wax is trickled onto cloth, making delicate shapes of lines and dots. The cloth is then dipped into dye. Wherever there is wax on the cloth, the dye doesn't soak in, and in this way a pattern forms. After the first dye bath, the wax is scraped off and new patterns are applied. The cloth is dyed again, to build up a more complicated design.

This piece of cloth was dyed using the *batik* method, and comes from the island of Java, in Indonesia, where some of the world's most beautiful *batik* fabric is made.

Malaysian skyscrapers

The Petronas Towers, in Malaysia's capital city, Kuala Lumpur, are among the tallest buildings in the world. The towers are occupied mainly by offices, but are also part of a development containing stores, a concert hall and a park. Each tower has 88 floors and is topped by a slim spire, and the two towers are joined by a bridge halfway up, which is open for the public to visit. Malaysia is a mainly Muslim country, and so the design of the towers was strongly influenced by Islamic architecture. They look rather like the minarets on top of a mosque.

The Petronas Towers, two of the world's tallest buildings, light up the skyline of Kuala Lumpur, capital city of Malaysia.

Singapore's mixture of styles

The tiny country of Singapore is home to people whose ancestors came to the island from all over Asia, as well as Europe. The styles of traditional architecture in Singapore have been influenced by the Chinese, Indians, Malays and British, or sometimes a mixture. Today there are also many modern, hi-tech office buildings and shopping malls.

Here you can see a row of Chinese-style buildings in Singapore, right in front of the island's biggest Muslim place of worship, the Sultan Mosque.

Indonesian puppets

Indonesian *wayang kulit* shadow puppet shows are performed against a cloth screen, lit from behind by a coconut oil lamp. They are based on long, famous Indian tales called the *Ramayana* and the *Mahabharata*. A single person controls over 20 different puppets, and he also provides all their voices, sings songs, and signals to the orchestra behind him to tell them what to play. Some shows are very long and the puppeteer may have to sit cross-legged for many hours.

An Indonesian shadow puppet like this one is made of a piece of leather, cut into intricate, lacy patterns.

INTERNET LINK

For a link to a website with a behind-the-screen look at Indonesian shadow puppets and clips of Indonesian music, go to **www.usborne-quicklinks.com**

71

Map makers can produce
extremely accurate maps by
studying satellite views of the Earth's
surface. This satellite image shows the
River Lena splitting into many channels
as it nears the Arctic Ocean. The river is
shown in dark blue and the land is green.

Maps of Asia

On the following pages you can see environmental maps of Asia which show different types of landscape such as desert, mountain and forest. They also show borders between countries, as well as capital cities and other major cities and towns.

North is at the top of every map. The grid lines on the maps are latitude and longitude lines, measured in degrees (°) and minutes (´). These lines are used to pinpoint the exact location of any spot on the Earth's surface. Latitude lines run around the globe, or side-to-side on a map. Important lines of latitude are named, such as the equator (0°), the Tropic of Cancer (23°27´N) and the Arctic Circle (66°30´N). Lines of longitude run from north to south, or from top to bottom on a map.

The maps have numbered and lettered grids. If you look up a place or feature in the map index on page 90, you will find page numbers and grid references to help you find it on a map. All the maps have scale bars to tell you the real distance that is represented by a distance on the map. Each map also has a key to explain the shading and symbols.

Here is an explanation of the different kinds of land cover shown by the map keys:

Boreal forest is cold forest, also called *taiga*. It's made up mainly of evergreen trees.

Temperate forest has a cool and a warm season, and trees there seasonally lose all their leaves.

Tropical forest is found near the equator. It's always hot there, with rain nearly every day.

Temperate grassland has a cool season and a warm season. Few trees grow there.

Savanna is hot grassland that receives very little rain, and so there are hardly any trees.

Semi-desert and scrub is a dry zone where only a few small bushes and plants can grow.

Hot desert has scarcely any rain at all, and may be covered in sand, gravel or rock.

Wetland is covered in marsh or swamp, and is often flooded or waterlogged.

Mountain is very high, rocky land. Many peaks together form mountain ranges.

Tundra is land where the ground is frozen nearly all year round and no trees grow.

Ice can be either land with a permanent ice cap, or enormous sheets of sea ice.

Cultivation is land used for farming, where people grow crops or keep animals.

RUSSIA AND CENTRAL ASIA

60°   2   80°   1

A

Svalbard
(Norway)   20°

B

40°   Franz Josef
Land

C

60°

D

80°

A R C

UNITED
KINGDOM
London

*North
Sea*

*Norwegian
Sea*

Arctic Circle

NORWAY
Oslo

North Cape

*Barents
Sea*

Novaya
Zemlya

Paris

NETHERLANDS

BELGIUM

LUXEMBOURG

FRANCE

DENMARK

SWEDEN

○ Murmansk

Kola
Peninsula

*Kara
Sea*

GERMANY

Berlin

*Baltic
Sea*

Stockholm

FINLAND

Helsinki

Lake
Ladoga

○ Arkhangelsk

3

CZECH
REPUBLIC

AUSTRIA

POLAND

LITHUANIA

ESTONIA

Lake
Onega

○ St. Petersburg

○ Vorkuta

SLOVAKIA

Warsaw

LATVIA

Vilnius

Budapest

HUNGARY

Minsk

BELARUS

○ Lviv

○ Cherepovets

Moscow

○ Ukhta

Ural Mountains

Ob

○ Novyy Urengoy

ROMANIA

Kiev

MOLDOVA

UKRAINE

Chisinau

○ Ryazan

○ Nizhniy Novgorod

Volga

West Siberian

Plain

○ Surgut

Ob

Yenisey

○ Odesa

Kharkiv ○

○ Voronezh

○ Kazan

Perm ○

○ Dnipropetrovsk

○ Simferopol

*Black
Sea*

○ Rostov

Volgograd

Krasnodar

Volga

○ Samara

○ Yekaterinburg

Irtysh

○ Chelyabinsk

R   **U**

40°
N

Ankara

TURKEY

○ Adana

Mount Elbrus
5,642m
(18,510ft)

GEORGIA

○ Astrakhan

○ Oral

○ Orenburg

○ Aqtobe

○ Atyrau

KAZAKHSTAN

○ Omsk

○ Tomsk

Krasno

○ Novosibirsk

○ Pavlodar

Astana

○ Barnaul

Tbilisi

ARMENIA
Yerevan

AZERBAIJAN
Baku

○ Tabriz

Caspian Sea

○ Aqtau

Aral
Sea

○ Qyzylorda

○ Qaraghandy

○ Balqash

○ Uskemen

○ Altay

○ Aleppo

SYRIA

○ Mosul

Baghdad

IRAQ

Damavand
5,604m
(18,386ft)

Tehran

○ Nukus

○ Dasoguz

TURKMENISTAN

UZBEKISTAN

Lake
Balkhash

○ Almaty

○ Urumqi

4

Ashgabat
(Ashkhabad)

○ Turkmenabat

Tashkent

○ Shymkent

Bishkek

KYRGYZSTAN

○ Osh

Tien Shan

○ Aksu

Tarim Basin

○ Ahvaz

○ Esfahan

○ Mashhad

○ Samarqand

Dushanbe

TAJIKISTAN

Kuwait City

KUWAIT

IRAN

○ Shiraz

○ Herat

○ Mazar-e Sharif

Taklimakan Desert

**SAUDI
ARABIA**

*Persian
Gulf
(The Gulf)*

○ Bandar-e
Abbas

AFGHANISTAN

K2
8,611m
(28,251ft)

○ Hotan

Riyadh

Manama

○ Zahedan

Kabul

○ Kandahar

Islamabad

○ Srinagar

QATAR

Doha

Abu Dhabi

PAKISTAN

○ Lahore

INDIA

Indus

Plateau of Tibet

C   60°E   D   80°   E

ALASKA 60°
(U.S.A.)

*Chukchi
Sea*

J

160°

H

140°

*East Siberian
Sea*

G

120°

*Wrangel
Island*

Arctic Circle

*St. Lawrence
Island*

*Gulf of
Anadyr*

Bering Sea

○ Anadyr

*New Siberia
Islands*

* ya*

Laptev Sea

*yr
sula*

3

*Aleutian Islands
(U.S.A.)*

Verkhoyansk

Kolyma Range

*Kamchatka
Peninsula*

2,959m
(9,708ft)

Range

○ Magadan

○ Petropavlovsk-Kamchatskiy

Lena

○ Yakutsk

al Siberian

Plateau

Lena

*Sea of
Okhotsk*

PACIFIC

OCEAN

40°
N

I   A

○ Tynda

Komsomolsk ○

Amur

Kuril Islands

Sakhalin

Yuzhno Sakhalinsk ○

Blagoveshchensk ○

○ Khabarovsk

*Lake
Baikal*

Jiamusi ○

Hokkaido

Irkutsk ◉ ○ Ulan Ude

Sapporo ◉

○ Manzhouli

○ Hakodate

JAPAN

■ **Ulan Bator**

Vladivostok ◉

*Sea of
Japan*

Sendai ○

Changchun ○

○ Chongjin

Honshu

MONGOLIA

4

tains

Gobi Desert

RUSSIA AND CENTRAL ASIA

The Great Wall of China

Baotou ○

■ **Beijing**

Boreal forest	Wetland	■ National capital
Temperate forest	Mountain	◉ Major city or town
Tropical forest	Tundra	○ Other town
Temperate grassland	Ice	See also main key
Savanna	Cultivation	on page 73.
Semi-desert and scrub		
Hot desert		
▬ International boundary		

Great Wall of China

*Qinghai
Lake*

○ Lanzhou

Huang He (Yellow)

▲ 2,490m
(7,988ft)   Height above or
below sea level

1:24,000,000

HINA

Zhengzhou ○

0   400   800km
0   200   400   600 miles

PAKISTAN

Zabol
Zahedan
Kerman
Sirjan
Iranshahr
Shiraz
Persepolis
Bushehr
Busher
Bandar-e Abbas
Abadan
Basra
An Nasiriyah

Panjgur
Turbat

Gulf of Oman

Tropic of Cancer

Sur

Masirah Island

Arabian Sea

INDIAN
OCEAN

H

G

Muscat

OMAN

Strait of Hormuz
OMAN
Suhar
Dubai
Sharjah
Al Ayn

Salalah

Socotra
(Yemen)

Cape Guardafui

F

UNITED ARAB
EMIRATES

Abu Dhabi
Doha
Manama
QATAR
BAHRAIN

Persian Gulf
(The Gulf)

Kuwait City
KUWAIT

Ad Dammam
Al Mubarrez
Haradh

Buraydah

Hail

Riyadh

A r a b i a n
P e n i n s u l a

R u b '   a l   K h a l i
(E m p t y   Q u a r t e r   )

SAUDI ARABIA

YEMEN

Al Mukalla

Hadhramaut

Gulf of Aden

SOMALIA

Hargeysa
Berbera

Marib

Najran
Sadah
Sana
Dhamar
Ibb
Taizz
Aden

3,760m
(12,336ft)

Bab al Mandab

DJIBOUTI
Djibouti
Dikhil

Dire Dawa

Abha
3,133m
(10,279ft)

A s i r

Al Hudaydah

Assab

ETHIOPIA
Dese

Medina

Mecca
At Taif

Jedda

Farasan
Islands

Karora

Dahlak
Archipelago
Massawa
Keren
Asmara

ERITREA

Teseney

Kassala

-116m
(-381ft)

Mekele
Ras Dashen
4,620m
(15,157ft)
Gonder
Bahir Dar
Lake Tana

*Ethiopian
Highlands*

Blue Nile

H e j a z

R e d   S e a

Port Sudan

SUDAN

Nubian Desert

Atbara

Wad Medani
Gedaref

Nile

Lake
Nasser

ISRAEL
JORDAN
Beer Sheva
Petra
Al Aqabah
Maan
Tabuk
Sharm el Sheikh
Hurghada

Port Said
El Mansura
Ismailia
Suez Canal
Suez
Cairo
Pyramids of Giza
Beni Suef
El Minya
Asyut
Sohag
Qena
Luxor
Valley of
the Kings

Mount
Sinai
2,285m
(7,497ft)
Sinai

*Arabian
Desert*

EGYPT

Aswan
Aswan High Dam
Tropic of Cancer

Nile

77

1 2 3 4

45° N

95° 90° 85° 80° 75° 70° 65°E 45° N

30° 35°

H C B A

MONGOLIA

Altay

Altai Mountains

Moguo Caves

CHINA

Qaidam Basin

Golmud

Hami

Turpan Depression
-154m (-505ft)
Turpan

Lop Lake

Urumqi
Shihezi

Altun Mountains

Salween

Nam Lake

Lhasa

Thimphu
BHUTAN

Plateau of Tibet

TIBET

Brahmaputra

Dibrugarh
Jorhat

Brahmaputra

Altay

Dzungarian Basin

Korla

Bosten Lake

Darjeeling

Biratnagar

Mount Everest
8,850m (29,035ft)

Kathmandu

Kluytup

Tien

Karamay

Kunlun Mountains

Tarim Basin

Taklimakan Desert

Hotan

Siling Lake

NEPAL

Pokhara

Gorakhpur

Kathmandu

Lake Zaysan

Yining

Shan

Pik Pobedy
7,439m (24,406ft)
Aksu

Lucknow

Kanpur

Almaty

Karakol

Lake Issyk

Karakorum Range

Indus

Kashi

Kongur Shan
7,719m (25,325ft)

K2
8,611m (28,251ft)

JAMMU AND KASHMIR

Gilgit

Srinagar

Bareilly

Ganges

Saharanpur

Meerut

Chandigarh

Aligarh

Agra
Taj Mahal

Gwalior

Balqash

Lake Balkhash

Taldyqorghan

Bishkek

Kara-Balta

KYRGYZSTAN

Jalal-Abad

Osh

Ludhiana

Delhi

New Delhi

Jaipur

Ajmer

KAZAKHSTAN

Qyzylorda

Shieli

Turkistan

Shymkent

Taraz

Namangan
Angren

Fargona

Khujand

TAJIKISTAN
Dushanbe

Communism Peak
7,495m (24,590ft)
Khorugh

Kulob

Hindu Kush

Jammu

Sialkot
Gujranwala

Amritsar

Lahore

Gujrat

Peshawar

Islamabad

Sargodha

Faisalabad

Sahiwal

Multan

Bikaner

Jodhpur

Ajmer

Shelek

Tashkent

UZBEKISTAN

Navoiy

Samarqand

Jizzax

Bixoro

Qurghonteppa

Konduz

Mazar-e Sharif

Kabul

Jalalabad

Kandahar

5,143m (16,873ft)

Quetta

Dera Ghazi Khan

Bahawalpur

Rahimyar Khan

PAKISTAN

Thar Desert

Larkana

Sukkur

Indus

Nawabshah

Urganch

Amu Darya

Syr Darya

Aral Sea

TURKMENISTAN

Turkmenabat

Mary

AFGHANISTAN

Helmand

Herat

5

78

BURMA (MYANMAR)

Monywa
Pye
Irrawaddy
Mount Victoria ▲ 3,053m (10,016ft)
Sandoway
Pathein
Sittwe
Mouths of the Irrawaddy

BANGLADESH
Khulna
Chittagong
Mouths of the Ganges

Bay of Bengal

Ranchi
Jamshedpur
Kolkata (Calcutta)
Sambalpur
Cuttack
Brahmapur
Vishakhapatnam
Rajahmundry
Vijayawada

Andaman Islands (India)
Port Blair
Little Andaman
Ten Degree Channel

Nicobar Islands (India)

INDIAN OCEAN

SRI LANKA
Trincomalee
Kandy
Sri Jayewardenepura Kotte
Colombo
Galle
Negombo
Jaffna
Mannar
Gulf of Mannar
Palk Strait

Nellore
Chennai (Madras)
Bangalore
Salem
Coimbatore
Tiruchirappalli
Madurai
Mysore
Davangere
Kochi (Cochin)
Trivandrum
Kozhikode (Calicut)
Mangalore

Eastern Ghats
Western Ghats

Deccan Plateau

Hyderabad
Warangal
Gulbarga
Solapur
Nanded
Krishna
Godavari
Chandrapur
Nagpur
Amravati
Akola
Raipur
Jabalpur
Bhopal
Indore
Aurangabad
Dhule
Malegaon
Nashik
Kolhapur
Belgaum
Hubli
Pune
Mumbai (Bombay)
Surat
Vadodara
Ahmadabad
Narmada
Rajkot
Bhavnagar
Jamnagar
Porbandar

Kutch

Arabian Sea

MALDIVES
■ Male

INDIAN SUBCONTINENT

- Boreal forest
- Temperate forest
- Tropical forest
- Temperate grassland
- Savanna
- Semi-desert and scrub
- Hot desert
- Wetland
- Mountain
- Tundra
- Ice
- Cultivation

■ National capital
⊙ Major city or town
○ Other town
— International boundary

▲ 2,490m (7,988ft) Height above or below sea level

See also main key on page 73.

1:12,000,000

0   100   200   300 miles
0   200   400km

KAZAKHSTAN

Almaty
Lake Issyk

KYRGYZSTAN

▲ Pik Pobedy
7,439m
(24,406ft)

Aksu

Karamay
Yining
Kuytun
Shihezi
Urumqi
Korla
Turpan
Bosten Lake

Dzungarian Basin

Tien Shan

Altai Mountains

Altay

Bulgan

■ Ulan Bato

MONGOLIA

-154m
(-505ft)
Turpan Depression

Hami

40°N

Tarim Basin

Taklimakan Desert

Hotan

Lop Lake

Altun Mountains

Mogao Caves

Yumen

5,547m
(18,199ft)

The Great Wall of China

Gobi Desert

Baotou

Hoh

Wuhai

35°

Kunlun Mountains

Qaidam Basin

Golmud

Qinghai Lake

Xining

Huang He (Yellow)

Lanzhou

Yinchuan

T

4

Plateau of Tibet

CHINA

Mount Li
(Terracot
Xian

Baoji

30°

Siling Lake

TIBET

Nam Lake

Lhasa

Brahmaputra

Yushu

Chang Jiang (Yangtze)

Shiyan

Xia

Yichang

Himalayas

NEPAL
■ Kathmandu

▲ Mount Everest
8,850m
(29,035ft)

Darbhanga
Darjeeling

Patna
Biratnagar

Bhagalpur
Rangpur

INDIA

Ranchi
Asansol
Rajshahi
Sylhet

BANGLADESH

Tropic of Cancer

Dhaka ■

Kolkata
(Calcutta)

Khulna

Chittagong

Cuttack

Mouths of the Ganges

Bay of Bengal

INDIAN

OCEAN

■ Thimphu
BHUTAN

Ganges

Guwahati

Shillong

Imphal

Aizawl

Dibrugarh

Brahmaputra

Salween

Mekong

Chengdu

Gongga Shan
7,556m
(24,790ft)

Leshan

Luzhou

Chongqing

Chang

Zunyi

Huaih

He

Xichang

Chang Jiang (Yangtze)

Panzhihua

Guiyang

Myitkyina

Dali

Kunming

Guili

Liuzhou

Irrawaddy

Lashio

Monywa
Mandalay

Mount Victoria
3,053m
(10,016ft)

Sittwe

BURMA
(MYANMAR)

Taunggyi

Pyinmana

Sandoway

Pye

Henzada

Pathein

Pegu

■ Rangoon

Mouths of the Irrawaddy

Moulmein

Simao

Gejiu

Lao Cai

Phongsali

Son La

Louangphrabang

Mekong

Chiang Mai

THAILAND

Red

Nanning

Yulin

Thai Nguyen

■ Hanoi

Hai Phong

Gulf of Tonkin

Thanh Hoa

LAOS

■ Vientiane

Udon Thani

Vinh

VIETNAM

Zhan

Haiko

Hai

Sanya

Salween

Irrawaddy

80

Q

J 120° K 125° L 130° M 135° N 140° P 145° 45°N

Hailar

Hulun Lake

La Perouse Strait

Kuril Islands (Russia)

Yichun

Amur

Hegang

Jiamusi

Qiqihar

RUSSIA

Daqing

Asahikawa

Hokkaido Kushiro

Ulanhot

Harbin

Jixi

Sapporo

Tomakomai

2

Greater Khingan Range

Mudanjiang

Lake Khanka

Hakodate

40°

Xilinhot

MANCHURIA

Vladivostok

Aomori

Changchun

Jilin

Yanji

Nakhodka

Tongliao

Akita

Chifeng

Liaoyuan

Chongjin

Sea of Japan

Sendai

3

Fuxin

Fushun

Hyesan

Niigata

Fukushima

Shenyang

Kanggye

Kimchaek

Honshu

Jinzhou

Anshan

NORTH KOREA

Hamhung

Sikhote Alin Range

Zhangjiakou

Dandong

Utsunomiya

ng

Qinhuangdao

Sinuiju

Wonsan

Toyama

JAPAN

Tokyo

35°

Beijing

Tangshan

Korea Bay

Pyongyang

Kanazawa

Mount Fuji

Tianjin

Gulf of Chihli

Dalian

Nampo

Fukui

Shizuoka 3,776m

Shijiazhuang

Yantai

Seoul

Inchon

Suwon

Nagoya

(12,388ft)

Zibo

Weifang

Qingdao

Chongju

Kyoto

Hamamatsu

ndan

Taian

Yellow

Taejon

Taegu

Okayama

Osaka

4

ng He (Yellow)

Jining

Sea

SOUTH KOREA

Pusan

Hiroshima

Wakayama

ngzhou

Xuzhou

Grand Canal

Lianyungang

Kwangju

Korea Strait

Fukuoka

Matsuyama

Shikoku

ngshan

Yancheng

Kitakyushu

Cheju

Nagasaki

Kumamoto

30°

Nanjing

Hefei

Wuxi

Cheju

Kyushu

Tai Lake

Shanghai

Kagoshima

Wuhan

Chang Jiang (Yangtze)

Hangzhou

Anqing

Ningbo

EASTERN ASIA

Poyang Lake

Jinhua

East

Boreal forest

Nanchang

China

Amami

Temperate forest

5

Linchuan

Wenzhou

Sea

Tropical forest

sha

Temperate grassland

Nanping

Ryukyu Islands

Okinawa

Savanna

Semi-desert and scrub

Ganzhou

Yongan

Fuzhou

(Japan)

Hot desert

Quanzhou

Taipei

Chilung

Wetland

guan

Xiamen

Sakishima Islands

Tropic of Cancer

Mountain

6

Meizhou

Taichung

Changhua

Tundra

ton

Shantou

Yu Shan **TAIWAN**

Ice

zhou

Tainan 3,997m

Cultivation

Kaohsiung

(13,113ft)

■ National capital

Hong Kong (Xianggang)

Taiwan Strait

Batan Islands

PACIFIC

⊙ Major city or town

○ Other town

International boundary

20°

th China Sea

OCEAN

▲ 2,490m (7,998ft) Height above or below sea level

See also main key on page 73.

1:14,000,000

Luzon Strait

0 200 400km

Babuyan Islands

PHILIPPINES

0 100 200 300 miles

7

Laoag

Aparri

Luzon

Tuguegarao

115° J 120° K 125° L 130° M 135° N 15°

81

A   90°E   B   95°   C   100°   D   105°   E

Brahmaputra
Lhasa
Himalayas
Mount Everest
8,850m
(29,035ft)
NEPAL
Thimphu
Darjeeling **BHUTAN**
Biratnagar
INDIA
Gongga Shan
7,556m
(24,790ft) Leshan
Chengdu
Wanxian
Chongqing
Neijiang
Luzhou
Zunyi
Yibin
Xichang
Zhaotong
C H

Darbhanga
Bhagalpur
Rangpur
Guwahati
Shillong
Dibrugarh
Jorhat
Brahmaputra
Panzihua
Guiyang
Anshun

25°
N
Asansol
Rajshahi
Sylhet
BANGLADESH
Dhaka
Imphal
Myitkyina
Baoshan
Dali
Kunming

Jamshedpur
Kolkata
(Calcutta)
Khulna
Aizawl
Kaiyuan
Gejiu
Liu

3
Chittagong
Mouths of the Ganges
Lashio
Simao
Ha Giang
Lao Cai
N
Qinzhou

Monywa
Mandalay
Mount
Victoria
3,053m
(10,016ft)
**BURMA
(MYANMAR)**
Phongsali
Son La
Thai Nguyen
Hanoi

20°
Sittwe
Meiktila
Taunggyi
Mekong
Louangphrabang
Hai Phong

Bay of Bengal
Pyinmana
Pye
Salween
Chiang Mai
LAOS
Thanh Hoa
*Gulf of
Tonkin*

4
Sandoway
Henzada
Irrawaddy
Pegu
Thaton
Vientiane
Phitsanulok
Udon Thani
Vinh

Pathein
Rangoon
Moulmein
Nakhon Sawan
Khon
Kaen
Savannakhet
Hue
Da

15°
*Mouths of the
Irrawaddy*
THAILAND
Ubon
Ratchathani
Pakxe

I N D I A N
Nakhon Ratchasima
Attapu

O C E A N
Tavoy
Bangkok
Stoeng Treng
Angkor *Tonle Sap*
VIET
Qui Nh

5
*Andaman
Islands*
(India)
*Andaman

Sea*
Mergui
Pattaya
Batdambang
CAMBODIA
Buo
Thue

Port Blair
Prachuap
Khiri Khan
Kampong
Chhnang
Kampong
Cham
Da Lat

*Little
Andaman*
*Mergui
Archipelago*
Krong
Kaoh Kong
**Phnom
Penh**
Bien Hoa

10°
Ten Degree Channel
Chumphon
Kampong Saom
Long Xuyen
Mekong
Ho Chi Minh
(Saigon)

Gulf of Thailand
Can Tho

Bac Lieu

6
Nicobar Islands
(India)
Nakhon Si
Thammarat
Con Son

Hat Yai

5°
Banda Aceh
Alor Setar
Yala
Kota Bharu

7
Lhokseumawe
George Town
(Penang)
Gunung
Tahan
Kuala Terengganu

Sumatra
Langsa
Taiping
Ipoh
2,187m
(7,175ft)
MALAYSIA
Natun
Island
(Indonesi

INDONESIA

A   90°E   B   95°   C   100°   D   105°   E

F · G · 120° · 115° · J · 130° · K

Wuhan · Hefei · Nanjing · Nantong · Wuxi
Yichang · Huangshi · Anqing · Wuhu · Shanghai
Chang Jiang (Yangtze) · Tai Lake
Yueyang · Poyang Lake · Hangzhou
Dongting Lake · Nanchang · Ningbo

East China Sea

MAINLAND SOUTHEAST ASIA

Changsha
Zhuzhou · Linchuan
Wenzhou

Shaoyang
Hengyang · Nanping
Chenzhou · Ganzhou · Yongan · Fuzhou

Shaoguan · Quanzhou
Wuzhou · Zhangzhou · Xiamen
Canton (Guangzhou) · Meizhou · Changhua · Taichung
Xi Jiang · Shantou

Macau · Hong Kong (Xianggang)

Chilung
Taipei
TAIWAN
Tainan · Yu Shan 3,997m (13,113ft)
Kaohsiung

Ryukyu Islands (Japan)
Sakishima Islands
Tropic of Cancer

	Boreal forest
	Temperate forest
	Tropical forest
	Temperate grassland
	Savanna
	Semi-desert and scrub
	Hot desert
	Wetland
	Mountain
	Tundra
	Ice
	Cultivation
■	National capital
⊙	Major city or town
○	Other town
	International boundary
▲ 2,490m (7,988ft)	Height above or below sea level

See also main key on page 73.

1:12,000,000

0 · 200 · 400km
0 · 100 · 200 · 300 miles

Batan Islands
Luzon Strait
Babuyan Islands

Laoag · Aparri
Tuguegarao
Ilagan
Mount Pulog 2,930m (9,613ft)

Paracel Islands

Dagupan
Cabanatuan
Luzon
Olongapo · Quezon City
Manila
Lucena · Naga
Calapan · Legaspi
Mindoro
Masbate

Philippine Sea

PACIFIC OCEAN

South China Sea

Calamian Group
Masbate
Calbayog
Roxas · Samar
Panay · Tacloban
Iloilo · Bacolod
Taytay · Cebu

PHILIPPINES

Spratly Islands

Negros · Surigao
Palawan · Dumaguete · Bohol
Puerto Princesa · Butuan
Cagayan de Oro
Iligan
Sulu Sea · Pagadian · *Mindanao*
Davao

MALAYSIA
Zamboanga
Jolo
Sulu Archipelago
General Santos

Bandar Seri Begawan
BRUNEI
Miri
Tawau
Celebes Sea
Talaud Islands

INDONESIA
Borneo
Kota Kinabalu · Sandakan
Bintulu · Tarakan

120° · H · 125° · J · 130° · K

2
25°N
3
20°
4
15°
5
10°
6
5°
7

A 100°E **B** 105° **C** 110° **D** 115°

MARITIME SOUTHEAST ASIA

Boreal forest	Wetland	■ National capital	
Temperate forest	Mountain	⊙ Major city or town	
Tropical forest	Tundra	○ Other town	
Temperate grassland	Ice	See also main key	
Savanna	Cultivation	on page 73.	
Semi-desert and scrub			
Hot desert			
International boundary			

2,490m
(7,988ft) ▲ Height above or
below sea level

1:12,000,000

0   200   400 miles

0 100 200 300 miles

VIETNAM
○ Qui Nhon

South Chi[na]
Sea

○ Nha Trang

Spratly
Islands

THAILAND

Andaman
Sea

○ Hat Yai
○ Yala
⊙ Kota Bharu
○ Alor Setar
Banda Aceh ○
Lhokseumawe ○
George Town ⊙ (Penang)
○ Langsa
⊙ Medan
Pematangsiantar ○

○ Kuala Terengganu

M A L A Y S I A

⊙ Taiping
Gunung
Tahan
▲
2,187m
(7,175ft)
⊙ Ipoh
○ Kuantan

Kota
Kinabalu ○

Bandar Seri
Begawan
BRUNEI ■
Miri ○

○ Bintulu

■ **Kuala Lumpur**
Seremban ○
⊙ Melaka

Strait of Malacca

○ Johor Bahru
■ **Singapore**
SINGAPORE

Natuna
Islands

Anambas
Islands

○ Sibu

Tanjung

▲
2,988m
(9,803ft)

⊙ Kuching

Simeulue

Lake
Toba

○ Sibolga

Nias

0° Equator

S
u
m
a
t
r
a

○ Pekanbaru

Riau Islands

⊙ Pontianak

B o r n e o

Samari

Balikpapa

○ Padang

Gunung
Kerinci
▲
3,805m
(12,483ft)

⊙ Jambi

Bangka

⊙ Pangkalpinang

Karimata Strait

○ Palangkaraya

○ Banjarmasin

Martapura ○

Mentawai
Islands

⊙ Palembang

Bengkulu ○   Lahat ○

○ Baturaja

Belitung

G r e a t e r   S u n d a   I s l a n[d]
I N D O N E S I[A]

Java Sea

Tanjungkarang-
Telukbetung ○

Krakatoa
▲
813m
(2,667ft)
Serang ○
⊙ Bandung

Jakarta ■
⊙ Bogor

○ Tegal

⊙ Semarang

Le[s]

⊙ Surakarta
○ Surabaya

○ Cilacap
J a v a
⊙ Yogyakarta
⊙ Jember
Malang ○
Denpasar ○

Bali

Lomb
Ma

INDIAN

OCEAN

Christmas
Island
(Australia)

A 100°E **B** 105° **C** 110° **D** 115°

120° 125°

Luzon Cabanatuan
ongapo Quezon City
Manila Luzon
Lucena Naga
Calapan Legaspi
Mindoro
Masbate **PHILIPPINES**
Masbate Calbayog
Roxas *Samar*
Panay Tacloban
Taytay Iloilo Bacolod *P h i l i p p i n e*
Cebu *S e a*
erto Princesa *Negros*
Bohol Surigao
Dumaguete
Butuan
Cagayan de Oro
ulu Sea Pagadian Iligan
Mindanao
Davao
Zamboanga
Jolo General Santos
Sulu
Archipelago

C e l e b e s   S e a

Talaud
Islands

Sangihe
Islands

Manado

Gorontalo
Ternate
Halmahera

M o l u c c a
S e a
Peleng
Obi
Palu

Celebes *Sula*
Islands
Palopo
Buru *Ceram*
C e r a m   S e a
Kendari Ambon
Watampone
Buton
Ujung Pandang

B a n d a   S e a
F l o r e s   S e a

da Islands Wetar
Flores **Dili**
Ende **EAST TIMOR**
Sumba *Sawu Sea* *Timor*
Sawu Kupang
Roti
T i m o r   S e a

120° F 125° G

PACIFIC
OCEAN

Admiralty
Islands

J 140°E K 145° L 150° M Equator 155° N
0° 0°

4 Jayapura 4 1
Wewak *Bismarck Sea* *New Ireland*
Mount Wilhelm Rabaul
4,509m Madang *New Britain*
(14,793ft)
Mount Hagen **PAPUA NEW GUINEA**
New Guinea Lae
5 5 5
Kerema *Solomon Sea*
Gulf of *D'Entrecasteaux*
Papua *Islands*
10° **Port** 1:18,000,000 10°
Torres Strait **Moresby** 0 400km
Cape York
6 *Cape York* 6 2
Peninsula **AUSTRALIA** 0 200 miles

J 140°E K 145° L 150° M 155° N

5°
N

P A C I F I C **PALAU**

O C E A N

3

Morotai
Equator 0°

Biak

Sorong
Misool *Yapen*

Fakfak *Maoke Range*
Jayapura
New
Puncak Jaya *Guinea*
5,030m
(16,502ft)
5°
S

Aru
Islands

Tanimbar *Dolak*
Islands

A r a f u r a   S e a *Torres Strait*

10°

6

Darwin NORTHERN TERRITORY
130° H 135° J 140°

AUSTRALIA

130° H 135° 140°

85

Country facts and flags

The following pages list the 31 Asian countries that appear in this book, in alphabetical order. There are some key facts about each one, including its area, population (rounded to the nearest 1,000 people), capital city, main and official languages, type of government and the currency used there. Above each entry is the national flag.

AFGHANISTAN

Nationality: Afghan or Afghani
Area: 647,500 sq km
(250,001 sq miles)
Population: 28,717,000
Capital city: Kabul
Main languages: Dari, Pashtu
Government: transitional
Currency: 1 afghani = 100 puls

BANGLADESH

Nationality: Bangladeshi
Area: 144,000 sq km
(55,599 sq miles)
Population: 138,448,000
Capital city: Dhaka
Main languages: Bengali, English
Government: republic
Currency: 1 taka = 100 poisha

BHUTAN

Nationality: Bhutanese
Area: 47,000 sq km
(18,147 sq miles)
Population: 2,140,000
Capital city: Thimphu
Main languages: Dzongkha, Nepali
Government: monarchy
Currency: 1 ngultrum = 100 chetrum

BRUNEI

Nationality: Bruneian
Area: 5,770 sq km (2,228 sq miles)
Population: 358,000
Capital city: Bandar Seri Begawan
Main languages: Malay, English
Government: constitutional sultanate
(a type of monarchy)
Currency: 1 Bruneian dollar = 100 cents

BURMA (MYANMAR)

Nationality: Burmese
Area: 678,500 sq km
(261,970 sq miles)
Population: 42,511,000
Capital city: Rangoon
Main language: Burmese
Government: military dictatorship
Currency: 1 kyat = 100 pyas

CAMBODIA

Nationality: Cambodian
Area: 181,040 sq km
(69,900 sq miles)
Population: 13,125,000
Capital city: Phnom Penh
Main languages: Khmer, French
Government: constitutional monarchy
Currency: 1 new riel = 100 sen

CHINA

Nationality: Chinese
Area: 9,596,960 sq km (3,705,407 sq mil
Population: 1,295,330,000
Capital city: Beijing
Main languages: Mandarin Chinese, Cantone
other Chinese dialects
Government: Communist state
Currency: 1 yuan = 10 jiao

EAST TIMOR

Nationality: Timorese
Area: 15,007 sq km (5,794 sq miles)
Population: 998,000
Capital city: Dili
Main languages: Tetum, Portuguese, Indonesian, English
Government: constitutional monarchy
Currency: 1 US dollar = 100 cents

INDIA

Nationality: Indian
Area: 3,287,590 sq km (1,269,346 sq miles)
Population: 1,049,700,000
Capital city: New Delhi
Main languages: Hindi, English, Punjabi, Tamil, over 1,600 other languages and dialects
Government: federal republic
Currency: 1 Indian rupee = 100 paise

INDONESIA

Nationality: Indonesian
Area: 1,919,440 sq km (741,100 sq miles)
Population: 234,893,000
Capital city: Jakarta
Main languages: Indonesian, English, Javanese
Government: republic
Currency: 1 Indonesian rupiah = 100 sen

JAPAN

Nationality: Japanese
Area: 377,835 sq km (145,883 sq miles)
Population: 127,214,000
Capital city: Tokyo
Main language: Japanese
Government: constitutional monarchy
Currency: 1 yen = 100 sen

KAZAKHSTAN

Nationality: Kazakhstani
Area: 2,717,300 sq km (1,049,155 sq miles)
Population: 16,764,000
Capital city: Astana
Main languages: Kazakh, Russian
Government: republic
Currency: 1 Kazakhstani tenge = 100 tiyn

KYRGYZSTAN

Nationality: Kyrgyzstani
Area: 198,500 sq km (76,641 sq miles)
Population: 4,895,000
Capital city: Bishkek
Main languages: Kyrgyz, Russian
Government: republic
Currency: 1 Krygyzstani som = 100 tyiyn

LAOS

Nationality: Lao or Laotian
Area: 236,800 sq km (91,429 sq miles)
Population: 5,922,000
Capital city: Vientiane
Main languages: Lao, French
Government: Communist state
Currency: 1 new kip = 100 at

MALAYSIA

Nationality: Malaysian
Area: 329,750 sq km (127,317 sq miles)
Population: 23,095,000
Capital city: Kuala Lumpur
Main languages: Malay, English, Mandarin Chinese, other Chinese dialects, Tamil
Government: constitutional monarchy
Currency: 1 ringgit = 100 sen

MALDIVES

Nationality: Maldivian
Area: 300 sq km (116 sq miles)
Population: 330,000
Capital city: Male
Main languages: Maldivian, English
Government: republic
Currency: 1 rufiyaa = 100 laari

MONGOLIA

Nationality: Mongolian
Area: 1,565,000 sq km
(604,250 sq miles)
Population: 2,712,000
Capital city: Ulan Bator
Main language: Khalkha Mongol
Government: republic
Currency: 1 tugrik = 100 mongos

NEPAL

Nationality: Nepalese
Area: 140,800 sq km
(54,363 sq miles)
Population: 26,470,000
Capital city: Kathmandu
Main language: Nepali
Government: constitutional monarchy
Currency: 1 Nepalese rupee = 100 paisa

NORTH KOREA

Nationality: Korean
Area: 120,540 sq km
(46,541 sq miles)
Population: 22,446,000
Capital city: Pyongyang
Main language: Korean
Government: authoritarian socialist
Currency: 1 North Korean won = 100 chon

PAKISTAN

Nationality: Pakistani
Area: 803,940 sq km (310,403 sq miles)
Population: 150,695,000
Capital city: Islamabad
Main languages: Punjabi, Sindhi,
Siraiki, Pashtu, Urdu
Government: federal republic
Currency: 1 Pakistani rupee = 100 paisa

PHILIPPINES

Nationality: Philippine
Area: 300,000 sq km
(115,831 sq miles)
Population: 84,620,000
Capital city: Manila
Main languages: Filipino, Tagalog, English
Government: republic
Currency: 1 Philippine peso = 100 centavos

RUSSIA

Nationality: Russian
Area: 17,075,200 sq km
(6,592,772 sq miles)
Population: 144,526,000
Capital city: Moscow
Main language: Russian
Government: federal government
Currency: 1 ruble = 100 kopeks

SINGAPORE

Nationality: Singaporean
Area: 693 sq km (268 sq miles)
Population: 4,609,000
Capital city: Singapore
Main languages: Mandarin Chinese, other
Chinese dialects, Malay, English, Tamil
Government: parliamentary republic
Currency: 1 Singapore dollar = 100 cents

SOUTH KOREA

Nationality: Korean
Area: 98,480 sq km
(38,023 sq miles)
Population: 48,289,000
Capital city: Seoul
Main language: Korean
Government: republic
Currency: 1 South Korean won = 100 chun

SRI LANKA

Nationality: Sri Lankan
Area: 65,610 sq km (25,332 sq miles)
Population: 19,742,000
Capital cities: Colombo/
Sri Jayewardenepura Kotte
Main languages: Sinhala, Tamil, English
Government: republic
Currency: 1 Sri Lankan rupee = 100 cents

TAIWAN

Nationality: Taiwanese
Area: 35,980 sq km
(13,892 sq miles)
Population: 22,500,000
Capital city: Taipei (Taibei)
Main languages: Taiwanese, Mandarin
Chinese, other Chinese dialects
Government: democracy
Currency: 1 new Taiwan dollar = 100 cents

TAJIKISTAN

Nationality: Tajikistani
Area: 143,100 sq km
(55,251 sq miles)
Population: 6,864,000
Capital city: Dushanbe
Main languages: Tajik, Russian
Government: republic
Currency: 1 Tajikistani somoni
= 100 tanga

THAILAND

Nationality: Thai
Area: 514,000 sq km
(198,457 sq miles)
Population: 64,265,000
Capital city: Bangkok
Main languages: Thai, English
Government: constitutional monarchy
Currency: 1 baht = 100 satang

TURKMENISTAN

Nationality: Turkmen
Area: 488,100 sq km
(188,456 sq miles)
Population: 4,776,000
Capital city: Ashgabat (Ashkhabad)
Main languages: Turkmen, Russian
Government: republic
Currency: 1 Turkmen manat = 100 tenesi

UZBEKISTAN

Nationality: Uzbekistani
Area: 447,400 sq km
(172,742 sq miles)
Population: 25,982,000
Capital city: Tashkent
Main languages: Uzbek, Russian
Government: republic
Currency: 1 Uzbekistani sum = 100 tyyn

VIETNAM

Nationality: Vietnamese
Area: 329,560 sq km (127,244 sq miles)
Population: 81,625,000
Capital city: Hanoi
Main languages: Vietnamese,
French, English
Government: Communist state
Currency: 1 new dong = 100 xu

United Nations

All the Asian countries except
for Taiwan (whose independent
status is disputed by China)
belong to the United Nations.
This organization brings
countries together to work
for peace and development.

ASEAN

Ten countries in southeastern
Asia – Laos, Burma (Myanmar),
Cambodia, Indonesia, Brunei,
Philippines, Malaysia, Thailand,
Singapore and Vietnam – belong
to the Association of Southeast
Asian Nations (ASEAN). They
work together for economic
growth, cultural development,
and to promote peace between
the countries in the region.

The ASEAN flag features a
bundle of ten rice stalks, which
represents the member countries
bound together in friendship.

INTERNET LINKS

For a link to a website where you
can find out more about cultures and
religions in many Asian countries, go
to **www.usborne-quicklinks.com**

89

Map index

This is an index of the places and features named on the maps on pages 74–85. Each entry is made up of the following parts: the name (in **bold** type), the country or region within which it is located (in *italics*), the page on which the name can be found (in **bold** type) and the grid reference (also in **bold** type). For some names, there is also a description explaining what kind of place it is, for example a country or national capital. To find a place on a map, first find the map indicated by the page reference, then use the grid to find the square containing the name.

A

Abadan, *Iran,* **77 E5**
Abakan, *Russia,* **74 E3**
Abha, *Saudi Arabia,* **77 D8**
Abu Dhabi, *United Arab Emirates, national capital,* **74 C4, 77 F7**
Abu Kamal, *Syria,* **76 D5**
Adana, *Turkey,* **74 B4, 76 C4**
Ad Dammam, *Saudi Arabia,* **77 F6**
Aden, *Yemen,* **77 E9**
Aden, Gulf of, *Africa/Asia,* **77 E9**
Admiralty Islands, *Papua New Guinea,* **85 L4**
Afghanistan, *Asia, country,* **74 D4, 76 H5, 78 A4**
Agra, *India,* **78 D5**
Ahmadabad, *India,* **79 C6**
Ahvaz, *Iran,* **74 C4, 77 E5**
Aizawl, *India,* **79 G6, 80 D6, 82 B3**
Ajmer, *India,* **78 C5**
Akita, *Japan,* **81 P3**
Akola, *India,* **79 D6**
Aksu, *China,* **74 E3, 78 E2, 80 B2**
Al Amarah, *Iraq,* **77 E5**
Al Aqabah, *Jordan,* **77 C6**
Alaska, *U.S.A.,* **75 K2**
Al Ayn, *United Arab Emirates,* **77 G7**
Aleppo, *Syria,* **74 B4, 76 C4**
Aleutian Islands, *North America,* **75 J3**
Al Hillah, *Iraq,* **76 D5**
Al Hudaydah, *Yemen,* **77 D9**
Ali Bayramli, *Azerbaijan,* **76 E4**
Aligarh, *India,* **78 D5**
Al Kut, *Iraq,* **77 E5**
Allahabad, *India,* **78 E5**
Almaty, *Kazakhstan,* **74 D3, 78 D2, 80 A2**
Al Mubarrez, *Saudi Arabia,* **77 E6**
Al Mukalla, *Yemen,* **77 E9**
Alor Setar, *Malaysia,* **82 D6, 84 B2**
Al Qamishli, *Syria,* **76 D4**
Altai Mountains, *Asia,* **74 E3, 78 G1, 80 D1**
Altay, *China,* **74 E3, 78 F1**
Altay, *Mongolia,* **78 H1, 80 E1**
Altun Mountains, *China,* **78 G3, 80 C3**
Amami, *Japan,* **81 L5**
Ambon, *Indonesia,* **85 G4**
Amman, *Jordan, national capital,* **77 C5**
Amravati, *India,* **79 D6**
Amritsar, *India,* **78 C4**
Amu Darya, *Asia,* **76 H4, 78 A3**
Amur, *Asia,* **75 G3, 81 M1**
Anadyr, *Russia,* **75 J2**
Anadyr, Gulf of, *Asia,* **75 K2**
Anambas Islands, *Indonesia,* **84 C3**
Andaman Islands, *India,* **79 G8, 82 B5**
Andaman Sea, *Asia,* **82 C5, 84 A2**
Angkor, *Cambodia,* **82 D5**
Angren, *Uzbekistan,* **78 C2**
Ankara, *Turkey, national capital,* **74 B4, 76 B4**
An Najaf, *Iraq,* **77 D5**
An Nasiriyah, *Iraq,* **77 E5**
Anqing, *China,* **81 J4, 83 G1**
Anshan, *China,* **81 K2**
Anshun, *China,* **82 E2**
Antalya, *Turkey,* **76 B4**
Aomori, *Japan,* **81 P2**
Aparri, *Philippines,* **81 K7, 83 H4**

Aqtau, *Kazakhstan,* **74 C3, 76 F3**
Aqtobe, *Kazakhstan,* **74 C3, 76 G1**
Arabian Desert, *Egypt,* **77 B6**
Arabian Peninsula, *Asia,* **77 E7**
Arabian Sea, *Asia,* **77 G8, 79 B6**
Arafura Sea, *Asia/Oceania,* **85 H5**
Arak, *Iran,* **76 E5**
Aral, *Kazakhstan,* **76 H2**
Aral Sea, *Asia,* **74 D3, 76 G2, 78 A1**
Arbil, *Iraq,* **76 D4**
Arctic Ocean, **74**
Ardabil, *Iran,* **76 E4**
Arkhangelsk, *Russia,* **74 C2**
Armenia, *Asia, country,* **74 C3, 76 D3**
Arqalyq, *Kazakhstan,* **76 J1**
Ar Ramadi, *Iraq,* **76 D5**
Ar Raqqah, *Syria,* **76 C4**
Aru Islands, *Indonesia,* **85 J5**
Asahikawa, *Japan,* **81 P2**
Asansol, *India,* **79 F6, 80 C6, 82 A3**
Ashgabat, *Turkmenistan, national capital,* **74 C4, 76 G4**
Ashkhabad, *Turkmenistan, national capital,* **74 C4, 76 G4**
Asir, *Saudi Arabia,* **77 D7**
Asmara, *Eritrea, national capital,* **77 C8**
Assab, *Eritrea,* **77 D9**
As Sulaymaniyah, *Iraq,* **76 E4**
Astana, *Kazakhstan, national capital,* **74 D3**
Astrakhan, *Russia,* **74 C3, 76 E2**
Aswan, *Egypt,* **77 B7**
Aswan High Dam, *Egypt,* **77 B7**
Asyut, *Egypt,* **77 B6**
Atbarah, *Sudan,* **77 B8**
Atbasar, *Kazakhstan,* **76 J1**
At Taif, *Saudi Arabia,* **77 D7**
Attapu, *Laos,* **82 E5**
Atyrau, *Kazakhstan,* **74 C3, 76 F2**
Aurangabad, *India,* **79 D7**
Australia, *Oceania, country,* **85 H6**
Austria, *Europe, country,* **74 A3**
Azerbaijan, *Asia, country,* **74 C3, 76 E4**
Azov, Sea of, *Europe,* **76 C2**
Az Zarqa, *Jordan,* **77 C5**

B

Bab al Mandab, *Africa/Asia,* **77 D9**
Babuyan Islands, *Philippines,* **81 K7, 83 H4**
Babylon, *Iraq,* **76 D5**
Bac Lieu, *Vietnam,* **82 E6**
Bacolod, *Philippines,* **83 H5, 85 F1**
Baghdad, *Iraq, national capital,* **74 C4, 76 D5**
Bahawalpur, *Pakistan,* **78 C5**
Bahir Dar, *Ethiopia,* **77 C9**
Bahrain, *Asia, country,* **77 F6**
Baikal, Lake, *Russia,* **75 F3**
Baku, *Azerbaijan, national capital,* **74 C3, 76 E3**
Bali, *Indonesia,* **84 E5**
Balikpapan, *Indonesia,* **84 E4**
Balkanabat, *Turkmenistan,* **76 F4**
Balkhash, Lake, *Kazakhstan,* **74 D3, 78 D1**
Balqash, *Kazakhstan,* **74 D3, 78 D1**
Baltic Sea, *Europe,* **74 A3**
Banda Aceh, *Indonesia,* **82 C6, 84 A2**
Bandar-e Abbas, *Iran,* **74 C4, 77 G6**

Bandar Seri Begawan, *Brunei, national capital,* **83 F6, 84 D2**
Banda Sea, *Indonesia,* **85 G5**
Bandung, *Indonesia,* **84 C5**
Bangalore, *India,* **79 D8**
Bangka, *Indonesia,* **84 C4**
Bangkok, *Thailand, national capital,* **82 D5**
Bangladesh, *Asia, country,* **79 F6, 80 C6, 82 A3**
Banjarmasin, *Indonesia,* **84 D4**
Baoding, *China,* **81 J3**
Baoji, *China,* **80 G4**
Baoshan, *China,* **82 C2**
Baotou, *China,* **75 F3, 80 G2**
Baqubah, *Iraq,* **76 D5**
Bareilly, *India,* **78 D5**
Barents Sea, *Europe,* **74 B2**
Barnaul, *Russia,* **74 E3**
Basra, *Iraq,* **77 E5**
Batan Islands, *Philippines,* **81 K6, 83 H3**
Batdambang, *Cambodia,* **82 D5**
Batumi, *Georgia,* **76 D3**
Baturaja, *Indonesia,* **84 B4**
Beer Sheva, *Israel,* **77 B5**
Beijing, *China, national capital,* **75 F4, 81 J3**
Beirut, *Lebanon, national capital,* **76 C5**
Belarus, *Europe, country,* **74 B3**
Belgaum, *India,* **79 C7**
Belgium, *Europe, country,* **74 A3**
Belitung, *Indonesia,* **84 C4**
Bengal, Bay of, *Asia,* **79 F7, 80 C6, 82 A3**
Bengkulu, *Indonesia,* **84 B4**
Beni Suef, *Egypt,* **77 B6**
Berbera, *Somalia,* **77 D9**
Berdyansk, *Ukraine,* **76 C2**
Bering Sea, *Asia/North America,* **75 K3**
Berlin, *Germany, national capital,* **74 A3**
Beyneu, *Kazakhstan,* **76 G2**
Bhagalpur, *India,* **78 F5, 80 C5, 82 A2**
Bhavnagar, *India,* **79 C6**
Bhopal, *India,* **79 D6**
Bhutan, *Asia, country,* **78 G5, 80 D5, 82 B2**
Biak, *Indonesia,* **85 J4**
Bien Hoa, *Vietnam,* **82 E5**
Bikaner, *India,* **78 C5**
Bintulu, *Malaysia,* **83 F7, 84 D3**
Biratnagar, *Nepal,* **78 F5, 80 C5, 82 A2**
Birjand, *Iran,* **76 G5**
Bishkek, *Kyrgyzstan, national capital,* **74 D3, 78 C2**
Bismarck Sea, *Papua New Guinea,* **85 L4**
Black Sea, *Asia/Europe,* **74 B3, 76 B3**
Blagoveshchensk, *Russia,* **75 G3**
Blue Nile, *Africa,* **77 C9**
Bogor, *Indonesia,* **84 C5**
Bohol, *Philippines,* **83 H6, 85 F2**
Bojnurd, *Iran,* **76 G4**
Bombay, *India,* **79 C7**
Borneo, *Asia,* **83 G7, 84 D4**
Bosten Lake, *China,* **78 F2, 80 C2**
Brahmapur, *India,* **79 E7**
Brahmaputra, *Asia,* **78 G5, 80 C5, 82 A2**
Brunei, *Asia, country,* **83 F7, 84 D3**
Budapest, *Hungary, national capital,* **74 A3**
Bulgan, *Mongolia,* **80 F1**

Buon Me Thuot, *Vietnam,* **82 E5**
Buraydah, *Saudi Arabia,* **77 D6**
Burma, *Asia, country,* **79 G6, 80 E6, 82 C3**
Bursa, *Turkey,* **76 A3**
Buru, *Indonesia,* **85 G4**
Bushehr, *Iran,* **77 F6**
Buton, *Indonesia,* **85 F4**
Butuan, *Philippines,* **83 J6, 85 G2**
Buxoro, *Uzbekistan,* **76 H4, 78 A3**

C

Cabanatuan, *Philippines,* **83 H4**
Cagayan de Oro, *Philippines,* **83 H6, 85 F2**
Cairo, *Egypt, national capital,* **77 B5**
Calamian Group, *Philippines,* **83 G5, 85 E1**
Calapan, *Philippines,* **83 H5, 85 F1**
Calbayog, *Philippines,* **83 H5, 85 F1**
Calcutta, *India,* **79 F6, 80 C6, 82 A3**
Calicut, *India,* **79 D8**
Cambodia, *Asia, country,* **82 E5**
Can Tho, *Vietnam,* **82 E6**
Canton, *China,* **81 H6, 83 F3**
Cape Gardafui, *Somalia,* **77 F9**
Cape York, *Australia,* **85 K6**
Caspian Depression, *Asia,* **76 F2**
Caspian Sea, *Asia,* **74 C3, 76 F3**
Caucasus Mountains, *Asia/Europe,* **76 D3**
Cebu, *Philippines,* **83 H5, 85 F1**
Celebes, *Indonesia,* **85 F4**
Celebes Sea, *Asia,* **83 H7, 85 F3**
Central Siberian Plateau, *Russia,* **75 F2**
Ceram, *Indonesia,* **85 G4**
Ceram Sea, *Indonesia,* **85 G4**
Chandigarh, *India,* **78 D4**
Chandrapur, *India,* **79 D7**
Changchun, *China,* **75 G3, 81 L2**
Changde, *China,* **80 H5, 83 F2**
Changhua, *Taiwan,* **81 K6, 83 H3**
Chang Jiang, *China,* **80 E4, 81 J4, 82 C2**
Changsha, *China,* **81 H5, 83 F2**
Changzhi, *China,* **81 H3**
Cheju, *South Korea,* **81 L4**
Chelyabinsk, *Russia,* **74 D3**
Chengdu, *China,* **80 F4, 82 D1**
Chennai, *India,* **79 E8**
Chenzhou, *China,* **81 H5, 83 F2**
Cherepovets, *Russia,* **74 B3**
Chiang Mai, *Thailand,* **80 E7, 82 C4**
Chifeng, *China,* **81 J2**
Chihli, Gulf of, *China,* **81 J3**
Chilung, *Taiwan,* **81 K5, 83 H2**
China, *Asia, country,* **75 E4, 78 G3, 80 E3, 82 E2**
Chisinau, *Moldova, national capital,* **74 B3, 76 A2**
Chittagong, *Bangladesh,* **79 G6, 80 D6, 82 B3**
Chongjin, *North Korea,* **75 G3, 81 L2**
Chongju, *South Korea,* **81 L3**
Chongqing, *China,* **80 G5, 82 E2**
Christmas Island, *Australia,* **84 C6**
Chukchi Sea, *Asia/North America,* **75 K2**
Chumphon, *Thailand,* **82 C5**
Cilacap, *Indonesia,* **84 C5**
Cochin, *India,* **79 D9**
Coimbatore, *India,* **79 D8**

93

General index

PHOTOGRAPHY CREDITS

Every effort has been made to trace the copyright holders of the material in this book. If any rights have been omitted, the publishers offer to rectify this in any future edition, following notification. The publishers are grateful to the following organizations and individuals for their contribution and permission to reproduce this material.

Cover(main) ©Dallas and John Heaton/CORBIS, (border) ©Bettmann/CORBIS; 1 ©Warren Marr/Panoramic Images/NGSImages.com; 2–3 ©J Yip/ImageState/Panoramic Images/NGSImages.com; 5(r) ©David Noton/Masterfile; 6–7 ©Yann Arthus-Bertrand/CORBIS; 10–11 ©Marc Garanger/CORBIS; 12(tr) ©Bryan & Cherry Alexander Photography/Alamy, (b) ©Dean Conger/CORBIS; 13(tr) ©Pat O'Hara/CORBIS, (b) ©Mark Newman/Lonely Planet Images; 14(l) ©Gregor Schmid/CORBIS, (br) ©Wolfgang Kaehler/CORBIS; 15(t) ©Jacques Langevin/CORBIS SYGMA, (b) ©Powerstock; 16(tl) ©Bettmann/CORBIS, (bl) ©Comstock Images/Alamy; 16–17(main) ©Anne M Peterson; 17(mr) ©Gideon Mendel/CORBIS; 18–19 ©David Edwards/National Geographic Image Collection; 20(t) ©Keren Su/CORBIS, (bl) ©Setboun/CORBIS; 21(tl) ©Dean Conger/CORBIS, (b) "Image courtesy of Earth Sciences & Image Analysis Laboratory, NASA, Johnson Space Center"; 22(t) ©Robert Patrick/CORBIS SYGMA, (bl) ©Roger Ressmeyer/CORBIS; 23(tr) ©Paul Howell/UNEP/Still Pictures, (bl) ©Michael S. Yamashita/CORBIS; 24(l) ©Orban Thierry/CORBIS SYGMA, (tr) ©Jon Spaull/CORBIS; 25(bl) ©Setboun Michel/CORBIS SYGMA, (r) ©David Samuel Robbins/CORBIS; 26(tr) ©Malie Rich-Griffith/Alamy, (bl) ©Paul H. Kuiper/CORBIS; 27(tr) ©Reza, Webistan/CORBIS, (b) ©Setboun/CORBIS; 28–29 ©Getty Images/Hilarie Kavanagh; 30(t) ©Getty Images/World Perspectives, (bl) ©ephotocorp/Alamy; 31(l) ©Getty Images/Peter Adams, (b) ©Getty Images/Alan Kearney; 32(main) ©Powerstock, (tr) ©Guido Alberto Rossi/tips images; 33(t) ©Pictures Colour Library, (br) ©Richard I'Anson/Lonely Planet Images; 34(tl) ©Getty Images/Andrea Pistolesi, (br) ©Jonathan Blair/CORBIS; 35(tr) ©David Samuel Robbins/CORBIS, (main) ©Getty Images/Nicholas DeVore; 36(bl) ©Chris Beall/Lonely Planet Images, (mr) ©www.hannahlevy.com; 36–37(main) ©www.hannahlevy.com; 37(ml) ©Chris Lisle/CORBIS; 38(tr) ©Robert Harding Picture Library/Alamy, (b) ©Hulton-Deutsch Collection/CORBIS; 39(main) ©Noshir Desai/CORBIS, 40–41 ©Getty Images/Harald Sund; 42(tr) ©Jose Fuste Raga/CORBIS, (b) ©Lui Liqun/CORBIS; 43(main) ©Getty Images/Keren Su, (br) ©Reza, Webistan/CORBIS; 44(tl) ©Peter Bowater/Alamy; 44–45(b) ©Michael S. Yamashita/CORBIS; 45(t) ©Pierre Perrin/CORBIS SYGMA, (b) ©Getty Images/Joseph Van Os; 46(l) ©Usborne, (mr) ©Royalty Free/CORBIS; 47(t) ©Getty Images/Michel Setboun, (b) ©SCPhotos/Alamy; 48(t) ©David Sanger Photography/Alamy, (b) ©Dallas and John Heaton/CORBIS; 49(t) ©Izzet Keribar/Lonely Planet Images, (br) ©Getty Images/D E Cox; 50(main) ©View Stock/Alamy, (tl) ©Bisson Bernard/CORBIS SYGMA; 51(tl) ©Jon Arnold Images/Alamy, (b) ©View Stock/Alamy; 52–53 ©Getty Images/Eric Meola; 54(tr) ©Michael S. Yamashita/CORBIS; 54–55(b) ©Nik Wheeler/CORBIS; 55(t) ©Getty Images/Geoffrey Clifford, (br) ©Glen Allison/Alamy; 56(main) ©Bohemian Nomad Picturemakers/CORBIS, (mr) ©Michael Freeman/CORBIS; 57(main) ©ImageState/Alamy, (b) ©Jack Fields/CORBIS; 58(t) ©Yvette Cardozo, (b) ©Jon Arnold Images/Alamy; 58–59(b) ©ML Sinibaldi/CORBIS; 60(main) ©Kevin R Morris/CORBIS, (tl) ©Getty Images/Carlos Navajas; 61(main) ©Getty Images/Hugh Sitton, (tl) ©Keren Su/CORBIS; 62–63 ©Robert Holmes/CORBIS; 64(tr) ©Paul Bigland/Lonely Planet Images, (bl) ©zefa/T. Allofs; 65(t) ©National Oceanic and Atmospheric Administration (NOAA), (br) ©Adrian Warren/Ardea.com; 66(main) ©Getty Images/Denis Waugh, (tr) ©Paul Almasy/CORBIS; 67(t) ©Neil Rabinowitz/CORBIS, (b) ©Photofusion Picture Library/Alamy; 68(main) ©Getty Images/Walter Bibikow, (tl) ©Paul A. Souders/CORBIS; 69 ©Getty Images/Hilarie Kavanagh; 70(l) ©Charles & Josette Lenars/CORBIS, (r)©Macduff Everton/CORBIS; 71(main) ©Shelly Gazin/CORBIS, (tl) ©Adrian Arbib/CORBIS; 72–73 ©NASA; 86–89 ©Flag Institute Enterprises Ltd; 89 (br) courtesy of ASEAN.

American editor: Carrie Armstrong; Website adviser: Lisa Watts; All maps ©Usborne Publishing.